The Coming of the Light

The Moonling Prince: Book Two

This far-future romance contains an empath, a reluctant prince, fine dining, hawkships, love, and betrayal.

by

Wendy Rathbone

Dedication

For Della, as always

1.

Someone with too much sparkling hair jewelry—not Ari's mother—said, thinking I could not hear, "…unbecoming. He glowers a lot. Well, I guess that's to be expected after everything he went through. Poor dear."

The standard banquet hall was always fancy, decorated with moon-lights strung about the ceiling, crystal chandeliers at each end, tables dripping with gold and purple cloths, fancy silver containers and plates, and platinum cutlery. It felt overly warm tonight.

I was glad Ari was late for dinner, because if he'd heard her he would've gone all dour for the entire meal, and it was not great fun to try to pull him out of his reveries and moods.

His moods. They happened a lot. It was going to take a long time for him to recover from twenty years of agony. My empath healing gift had taken away his pain, but for his mental anguish, and the grief of losing the spirit of his twin, all I could offer him was love because he had forbidden me to touch his emotions with my gift. He wanted to hold onto them, and was afraid I might be tempted to "heal" them because they gave him pain. Of course I would never do anything of the sort without his consent despite the nightmares he had nearly every other night. He'd wake quivering in the dark, confused. By morning he'd forget them.

I still did not know most of these people who came to evening meals. Strangers to me, they hung about the king and the palace. I had no idea about their jobs or their personalities, even though I'd been introduced to them by the king now and again.

I needed to pay more attention.

So much had happened so fast. I'd only been on the domed moon called Firgone for two months. More than two weeks of that I had spent in its main city, Xia, as dreary and beautiful a place as any gothic metropolis described in a dark myth.

For sixteen days I had lived in Xia, having run away from Ari, whom people referred to as the Moonling Prince now that he was healed and was in line again for the throne. He'd always officially been in that line, but he had been so non-functional after the splinter-bomb attack that decimated his realm's home world that no one ever believed he'd rule. In his condition, he'd been incapable of any regular lifestyle.

Now, all that had changed.

When Ari had finally found me in the looming depths and shadows of that moon-city, which I had fallen in love with and hoped one day to call my home, he had swept me off my feet the best he could, having had no experience with love or lovers save a couple of fumbled nights with me.

I allowed the sweep of course. He was all I wanted. Him, and only him. In all my experiences of healing, I had never fallen in love with one of my patients. Until Prince Arulu. Ari. The Moonling Prince of the Realm of the September Stars.

Ari was awkward, didn't always know what he wanted or how, but he was the most intriguing person I'd ever met, strangely beautiful in his predicament, his suffering, and all I wanted was to help him. And love him.

He'd accused me of taking away one agony and replacing it with another. Pain was the first. That second agony? For him, grief and love were entwined right now, and there was nothing to be done for it.

The king approached me from behind one of the long tables, alone, trailing traditional scarves of blue woven with lavender. His hair was often worn loose and down, but tonight it was elaborately braided in a hundred tiny snakes and they, in turn, were braided into a single plait along his back and tied with a black ribbon. I'd heard Ari refer to it as the Braid of Ruling.

"Is my son is not here?"

"Not yet. He's running late."

6

The king, who insisted everyone call him by his first name, Kean, nodded. In the time I had been on Firgone, he had said nothing to me about the time Arulu and I spent together, nor about our new living conditions, though he had to know about them. Escorts and king's spies were everywhere. But now he spoke. "You have been spending a lot of time together," Kean said. "The nights, too. Your things are moved into his rooms."

My voice caught in my throat. I didn't know what to say, afraid he thought I'd overstepped a boundary or two. This was his son. He'd only just gotten him back from the brink of hell.

Kean brushed at the air with his hand. "It's all right. I suppose you'll have vat-grown children. That's fine. It's all the rage right now."

I cleared my throat. Marriage? Was he talking marriage? I'd never even pictured myself in that scenario. My cheeks flushed. "Sir, with all due respect, it's only been a few weeks." *And your son has never asked, let alone hinted.*

The king, turned, gaze gentle. "Yes. But you're so good for him. I can see that."

"Thank you."

Kean smiled. "It is I who cannot thank you enough."

While lying in bed this morning, fingering a new, soft spread Ari had bought from the city, Ari had told me, much to my dismay, he had three goals in his new life:

Bring back the dead. Make the old starships fly again. Make love every day.

He said that as if it were all so simple, like a joke. And ruling was not in that mix.

He was still coming down from the throes of pleasure when he spoke, drunk on sex, on me. And all of it still mixed up with grief for his dead twin, Arku. He often spoke poetically while in that post-coital state. But he never spoke of marriage. Or kids, vat-grown or otherwise.

And he never mentioned Arku by name.

I looked at Kean and simply nodded.

I still saw myself lying next to Ari that morning, my skin heated and damp, our hips pressed, and my hands roaming over him and that new coverlet.

He'd noticed and said to me, "You like it? It is chintz. A very old material but soft against the skin."

I wasn't interested in the chintz, and kissed him. He'd leaned into it, then pulled back and touched my cheek.

"I want to go where it's snowing, and listen to the silence. It's winter right now in the southern hemisphere on the terraformed moon Darkquill. I want to take you there. In one of the hummingbird ships."

"If you like," I replied. I didn't care where I was as long as I could be with him.

How I adored the way Ari talked after lovemaking. Even if the courtier who'd called him "glowering" had been right in many ways— since he still suffered grief and nightmares—I would describe him more as glowing when we were alone together in his bedroom—our bedroom now—and learning each other's deepest thoughts.

Over the past couple of weeks I'd learned many things about him. He liked music and art. He liked drawing but refused to show me anything he'd done, saying he destroyed everything he tried to make half-way to the finish. I now knew he wanted to try to revisit childhood dreams. Become a starship designer. A star-boat engineer. He wanted to see all the other moons. Then he wanted to tour the galaxy in a home-made ship.

Ari had so many plans, other than ruling, now that the pain had left his body, and his mind was clear.

And my plans? I spent my days healing one or two small ailments in the palace, but with the fantastic medical technology of this realm my empath gift was not in much demand. Mostly, I was still trying to orient myself to the culture, and to having a new lover in my life.

A hush came over the banquet room, like a wave, bringing me out of my reverie. I looked up. Ari entered dressed in his favorite red and silver, which became him, off-setting the richness of his gold skin, his dark hair. People nodded toward him, a few nearest the door greeted him, and the noise of chatter resumed.

He still smiled rarely, but when he did it showed off his pearl-white teeth. Tonight he ignored the guests, scanned the room, and found me. His smile was all for me as he headed toward me rapidly, and my heartbeat increased just seeing him. Seeing the way he reacted to me was a thrill.

Maybe Kean hadn't had spies after all. The way Ari's eyes shone as he came up alongside me, and the heat that instantly flared between us so evident, how could everyone in the room not feel it as well and know immediately, seeing our faces and our body language, that we were two beings in love?

I smelled wildthorne on him, earthy, and a hint of sweetwind from the spray he used on his brown hair which hung glossy, unbraided, thicker against one side of his face than the other where it cascaded heavily over his right shoulder and down his back.

He reached out and touched my lower back with the open palm of his hand. I hadn't seen him since that morning, and that touch which I'd been craving sent flame through my stomach and abdomen. He said in a discreet whisper close to my ear, "I've been thinking about you all day."

"What about me?" I teased back.

"Let's just say it involved you wearing far less clothing than you're wearing right now."

I laughed.

Meat and bread scents wafted up as the servants brought out steaming food fresh from royal ovens. Ari and I took our seats next to Kean at the head of the table.

I had barely done anything strenuous today, but I was starving.

I had fallen in love with the palace, the black city it overlooked, and its crown prince. But I still was not quite used to all the luxuries. I had eaten in community dining rooms at the Onyx Temple where I was raised and taught how to use my empath gift, but while the Temple was a big place, it was not lavish as far as décor. We had plain white table cloths. Wooden furniture. Narrow beds with white sheets and black blankets and spreads. We wore black robes as adults most of the time. As girls and boys, we wore simple dark drawstring pants and white wrap shirts that tied in the front. We had games and toys like any children, and went to Temple school every day. But it was only after I left and came to the Realm of the September Stars that I realized how austere my upbringing had been. I never longed for luxury because I had all I needed.

But now I was still trying to get used to everything from fine clothes to fine foods in elaborate halls. I had no set schedule except for meals in the afternoon or evening with the king and queen. I was actually a bit adrift.

And I had never been in love before. All was strange and new.

There were so many things I was still learning. One thing I wanted to know more about was the recent history of these humans of Lyric Prime. They were brilliant artisans and scientists. They invented, and held patents on, strange stardrives that appeared to require no fuel, and no one could figure them out, even with reverse engineering.

Rumors bounded throughout the galaxy that they were sorcerers, witches, or religious fanatics who had learned to speak to the gods. I had seen no evidence of this so far, and in fact it was these people who looked at me, with my gift, as a sorcerer at times.

Curious, I found as much reading material as I could.

I'd been reading most of the day. I had lots of questions. But I was afraid to bring them up over dinner. Recent history was a touchy subject. Not appropriate dinner conversation.

Instead of thinking about that right now, I concentrated on eating the delicious food and listening to harmless palace chatter.

2.

Ari lay back in the bed under the dusky dome-light that flowed along the bed sheets and dappled across his smooth skin. The splendor of him, like gazing upon one of the Galactic Eight Wonders, could not be matched by any human I'd ever seen, or known.

After dinner, we'd rushed to his rooms and both shed our clothing in record time, climbing into the bed.

Now, I knelt beside him, running my hands all over his body. I lowered my head to nuzzle his throat. I never wanted to stop kissing all of him. Tasting all of him. It was as if he burned with an elixir special for me, made up of all my favorite things so that I would crave him, and continue to crave him until I felt I had to touch him, or die.

He moved into my arms, wonderful, warm, and turned his face to me wordlessly asking to be kissed, but still sometimes hesitant, overly unsure for a man his age. But I knew him now, and I knew why this was, and it wasn't strange at all.

Arms around my waist, he pulled me close. I pushed my right leg between his thighs, feeling his entire body against mine thrumming with life, need, passion.

As far as I knew, he had been a virgin on the first night we spent together. If we took things too fast, sometimes he still became shy.

I pulled back to stare into his face. The brown eyes shimmered, deep and vivid. I could see the individual lines of his thick lashes so dark, and the whites of his eyes clear and unblemished, unlike when I first met him and they had looked so tired of the pain, so bloodshot.

In the last few weeks his natural beauty had bloomed with the grace of renewed confidence. His shoulders unknotted. His chin was held higher showing off the strong family line he came from, all with the high cheekbones and smooth, unshadowed foreheads. He mesmerized me.

Now he smiled, showing a flash of teeth, and said, "You're looking at me like you don't believe I'm real."

"You're just—" I started to answer, but the words faded from my brain. "What you do to me," I finally finished.

My palm stroked over his shoulder, hard bone, muscle flexing, and down the gentle curves of muscles on his arm. Flawless. A treasure. Maybe he was right and I didn't believe he, or any of this, was real.

Coming here so fresh and new, my first time off-world or aboard a starship, was like a dream. Sometimes I had the passing thought: *When will I wake up?* The moon-palace could've been the setting of any dark fairy tale. The city of Xia was a witchy-looking place. And I'd fallen for the realm's prince-under-a-curse. These kinds of stories had been told over and over for millennia. In my mind, real people didn't actually inhabit them.

I ran my hand down his back and over the narrow hips to his backside. He moaned, pulling me into another kiss as my hand grew bolder, dipping gently into the warm crevice, feeling a light dusting of hair. Ari's body was mostly devoid of hair. Even at his crotch and under his arms it was thin, almost straight, and very black. He did not have to shave every day, and the dark shadow that slowly grew along his chin and jaw made him look more chiseled. If he shaved only every other day, then it was the second day I loved best when he looked the most compelling to me, because of that shadow. Like right now.

When my fingers brushed along the line between his buttocks, and I touched him a bit too intimately, he startled in my arms, body giving a slight jerk, and I moved my hand to his thigh. He did not stop kissing me, only held me tighter, pressing our erections together.

We'd never discussed taking our lovemaking further than rubbing, or sucking. I didn't mind. We were young. This was new.

I myself was no virgin, though. I had had full intercourse several times with Nik, trading who would be on top. When

Nik first told me about wanting to do that, he ducked his head as if afraid I'd reject him, and quickly added that many men did not prefer it and we did not have to do it. But I lived such a careful life in the Temple that when I was with Nik I craved adventure. I was unabashedly open to anything he suggested. I was ready to go for it quicker than he was.

With Ari, all instincts told me to move slowly.

He rolled half on top of me and kissed his way down my neck to my chest. The pleasure of that was like nothing I'd known before. This cursed prince. This beautiful man.

He moved his way down my body until he reached my groin. His mouth took me in, slow, hot, wet. I had to bite hard on my lip to keep from coming right away. He was easy on me for awhile, having been a quick learner on how to draw out pleasure, make it last, while at the same time driving me mad with lust. I sometimes thought I loved him more than he loved me, but when he did this with increasing skill every time, I had no fear that he actually adored me.

I put my hands gently on his shoulders, our wordless sign that I was peaking, and he increased the pressure and the speed with enthusiasm.

My mind went white. My breath caught in the back of my throat like a knot of wind leashed. The rims of my eyelids became damp. And my voice. My voice was lost in a tangled universe of ecstasy. Impending release. Like powering through impossible mazes forming puzzles that would take a million years to solve. And yet doing it with great ease because your beloved who is twin to your soul is gleefully showing you the way.

The tangles loosened and fell, the maze widened to a single, gilded path and the puzzle completed to a bright picture of unending light. All keys to all locks. Solutions. Answers. Wholeness.

Here and now. Release and ecstasy.

Ari soothed and comforted me, hands on my thighs, stomach, sides, until time reverted to human, space, breathing, lover.

He wiped his mouth on a towel we kept handy, still not keen on swallowing yet, but laughed as he came up to kiss me with the scent of me on his lips, the wine of love still moist in his mouth.

He allowed me time to recover, not too demanding, but I could feel him, eager, wanting. Strength flowed back into me and when I was steady again I flipped him onto his back. He crooked a knee, wrapping it about my thigh as if to hide himself, but finally fell all the way back with a sheepish grin and dropped his forearm over his eyes as I slowly trailed my tongue from throat to navel, circling it, eying the response as his organ drew up tighter, lightly patting his stomach. He was so lovely, impressively long and hard. He cocked his knee again, trying to turn. Eager or shy? It didn't matter. He was simply damn enticing. I knew when I put my mouth right over the head, he would lose all inhibition. His legs would open, his body would arch and he would groan under his breath in little, sweet gasps.

I licked toward my prize, but first put my hand lower, softly caressing his balls with my thumb and fingers.

Already his dark head was tossing on the pillow. I touched my tongue tip to the head, soft, laving him. He gave a yell and thrust up. Taking pity, I let my lips part so he could move into my mouth on his own. Then I closed my lips and sucked down.

I think he said my name a few times before he finally quieted and I could hear only the deep heaving of his breath as I went to work, taking time to make sure the pleasure lasted for him, knowing exactly how to tease and how to decrease or increase the urgency. How to make him come. Or not.

Finally, he desperately called my name. His hips came up and I knew he wanted me to take him over the edge, let go, let him fly. "Tahir," he said again. I circled his length with my tongue, touching all the areas I knew were most sensitive,

14

tickling, teasing, then sucking hard. He started to hyperventilate. When his body stiffened, his breathing stopped. He gave a strangled cry and came.

In many ways he was still like an adolescent, yet worse for it because he'd been held back by his condition for so many years. Pain had taken away his libido for the most part, but now he made up for it. His orgasms were strong and pure, and he seemed to pulse unabated for twice as long as I, his body at long last able to abandon itself to overdue pleasure. I grinned at him because it was more than I could swallow every time. He was quite potent.

We laughed about that sometimes, though his skin always flushed at the realization that he was so exuberant. Not wanting him to feel a moment's embarrassment, I distracted him afterward, morning and night, with more kisses.

We started a great routine. Once at night. Once in the morning if we woke early enough. We were quite happy. Quite sated.

Our infatuation with each other followed us afterward as we would continue to kiss until we fell asleep. Sometimes he'd curl against my shoulder. Sometimes I'd roll half on top of him as if, even in sleep, I was afraid he'd run away. Or maybe it was that I thought I could protect him from his nightmares.

Some nights he would twitch and moan. Sometimes he'd wake, other times not, but I always woke. I would stroke his forehead until he calmed.

I worried that the memory of the splinter-bomb and his brother's death, along with an abundance of pain for so many years, had made him too fragile for all the things his father was now demanding of him. I didn't think he was weak, on the contrary, a survivor like him was strong. But the stress of ruling a realm, along with ensuing politics, could deepen his mental scars. What if it got worse than simple nightmares? I knew side-effects for recovering from situations like his could involve PTSD, insomnia, dissociation, quick temper, depression, anxiety, and more. So far, he seemed to have avoided those things, aside from his grief. But it had only been a few weeks.

I did not study him like he was some specimen. I merely worried.

Tonight he seemed exhausted and fell asleep quickly. I moved over him and embraced him, resting my head on a pillow against his neck. I felt his breath feather against my hair, heard the drum of his heart. Luxuriating in the warmth and scent of him surrounding me, I entered a heavy sleep of my own.

*

Something woke me. The only light was the purple flashing from the dome, and the dim moons beyond. But for a moment I couldn't see even that, only a drowsy kind of dark. I heard labored breathing and felt its wind across my face. Familiar. Pleasant. Beloved.

Something hot against my cheek. A raspy voice. "Tahir."

I opened my eyes. Ari was leaning over my face, his hair curtaining around us. I could see the flash of his eyes, the darker shadow of his mouth, but not much else. The sweet fragrance of him which I loved now more than any other scent, caused me to arch up into him, still half-sleep.

Until I realized he was trembling. His breath short and fast.

I immediately woke all the way, my hands scrabbling up from the covers to cup on either side of his waist. His skin felt cool and tense, slightly damp. Shivers trembled him, the softness of him going coarse.

"Ari?"

"I—I—" He could not speak. He was soundlessly sobbing, breath wracked.

My hands moved up to his face, pushing back his hair. I could see the streaks of tears, lavender in the light. "Ari."

16

I tried to pull him down to me but he was balanced on his arms, stiff, unmoving. He managed to say, "They're mad about something."

"Who?"

His brow narrowed. His eyes rolled up and closed. Then he collapsed on top of me.

"Ari?" I brushed at his hair and the sides of his face.

His eyes opened, blinked. He said in a forlorn tone, "I don't know. I think I was dreaming."

I stroked my hand along his back. "You're awake now?"

He nodded, looking confused. "Sorry I woke you." He rubbed a hand across his eyes. "Was I crying?"

I gave him a gentle smile. "I don't know."

"Okay, then." He burrowed back into my shoulder and fell quickly back to sleep. I held him for awhile, wide awake. It had happened before but not quite like this. He usually said nothing, his sleepy eyes opening for a moment. By morning, he never remembered.

Finally, I fell back to sleep, with Ari's warm breath on my chest and his slippery cool body wrapped around me.

*

The next morning we had breakfast brought into the room. Ari ate more than usual, including a double helping of the most delicious pastry, then disappeared into his closet for awhile.

I idly crumbled a piece of toast until it looked like brown sand littering a beautiful china plate painted with a stone gargoyle looking up at a peach moon. It was now surrounded by brown toasted snowflakes of stars.

So much around me now was like that, art and luxury. Even the utensils had intricate embosses of trees, fruit, strange animals, dragons. Or the god Sinarha. The tablecloth for our breakfast meal was finest white lace inlaid with designs of male and female bodies entwined. The coffee pot was shaped like a colorfully plumed bird that was alien to me. Our food was always hot and fresh. Everything seemed to gleam.

Ari came out of the dressing room-closet wearing dark blue trousers, his white shirt still unbuttoned. He held an elaborate pink coat with lots of straps and buttons and buckles hanging from it.

I could not look away from the beautiful skin of his chest and throat even as he put the coat on a chair and idly began buttoning the shirt. His hair scattered everywhere, all over his shoulders and back, shining strands hanging in his face.

I got up and went to him, putting my arms over his shoulders. He stopped buttoning and grasped me in return, saying in mock irritability, "What?"

I kissed him in answer. He always looked fantastic. I told him so many times a day. But words got old.

When we broke apart, I put my hands against his chest and finished buttoning his shirt for him. Then I helped him into his coat.

"More meetings with Kean?" I asked.

He nodded, eyebrows narrowing.

I reached out and curled my fingers around a clump of his hair. "What about the hair?" Sometimes he pulled it all back into a wide comb. Or fastened the front parts into little black clips.

"What about it?" he asked.

"Nothing. It's always stunning, that hair of yours." When he wore it down I first thought he was just being lazy. But later I realized he was never more beautiful than when his hair was allowed to be wild. It was part of his personality formed from a rather savagely-shaped life up to now, once grasping at new and more intimate identities that had eluded his growth. His existence had been so utterly cruel. He was still waking from that.

The hair was a statement.

I wanted him to be open to me about that, about everything. I said, trying to keep my voice casual, "So, that nightmare you had last night seemed pretty bad. What was it?"

His smile dropped. He frowned. "Really? I don't remember." He turned away, grabbing for his coat. "My father is waiting. I'm already late. I'm sorry. I'll talk to you later."

"But Ari—"

He never talked of Arku. Not once since the day the ghost of his twin left. But I knew that ghost was what he dreamed.

At the door he turned. He gave me his rare smile. "Not that I regret being late. Spending mornings with you is wonderful, my father be damned."

I grinned at his words, forgetting what I was about to say. He was learning to express himself more and more every day. And, well, any compliment he made toward me left my heart desperately wallowing in my throat.

3.

A hubbub came from the hall, noises like pounding, voices. I walked out of the room to see garlands, streamers, gilt everywhere. People were on hover platforms decorating all up and down the halls. Obviously, a celebration was in the works. Ari had never mentioned it.

On my world, and back in the Temple, we had winter solstice with wreaths of sticks and husks, garlands of ribbons, and presents. This looked like something along those lines. But there were no seasons under the dome.

"What is this?" I asked a nearby servant.

"The Coming of the Light."

"What light?"

"Our moon does not have an axis so we don't have day or night. Our orbit is fixed about the sun. But every half-year we go from dark to light. We will face the sun for half a moon year now. The light comes tomorrow. It's a sight to behold. If you've never seen it before, well, it transforms the moonland into white plains and hills. The dome darkens to protect us from ultraviolet rays, but the whiteness never goes away, not for half a year."

I felt a bit stupid to not even think of that. Of course they would have half a year of light and half a year of dark.

I moved down the corridors and hallways mesmerized by the gold and red glass balls formed in all shapes from interlocked triangles and circles to jagged lines and spirals. Garlands draped the walls and ceilings in crystal necklaces. Tasteful and elegant.

Why hadn't Ari mentioned it?

I went in search of him, finding him just leaving the throne room with his father and the entourage.

The throne room was decked out in beautiful décor, mostly gold and silver garlands adorning the walls and the thrones. The tables had gold cloths. Bouquets of white flowers were everywhere, their fragrance like pure sugar pouring through the air.

Ari came over to me and said, "Come with us. We're going to the landing field."

I nodded to Arulu and fell into step beside him. "Why didn't you tell me about the Coming of the Light?"

"I thought you knew."

I shook my head. "I should've, maybe—"

He interrupted, frowning. "I keep forgetting you're still so new. You fit in so well here."

"Even so, you never mentioned it."

Ari said, "It means nothing to me. I hate it, actually, just a lot of pomp."

"You hate it?" Then I realized he would not have been well enough to enjoy ordinary things like this, even yearly festivities, and might have come to resent them.

"Yeah. It's stupid." His voice turned toneless.

20

I nodded, and said nothing more. But it got my mind thinking. For years, he couldn't abandon himself to pleasure like celebration, or even love, because his guard had always been up. Because he had had only horror, night after night, to look forward to, it made sense. Change was happening to him, and would continue to happen. But it would be slow.

I wanted to take his hand. More, I wanted to embrace him. But I didn't know how public he'd been about us. I didn't want to presume anything, despite the fact that the king knew and didn't seem fazed at all.

My impulse to touch was both my training kicking in, combined with my growing affection for him. When he closed in on himself, my instinct was to open.

I forced myself to keep up with him as he headed out of the palace, my fists clenched at my sides.

The light was pale blue and gray all around us.

"What's at the moon base?" I asked.

"Regents from the other nine moons are coming in," Ari said. "A big meeting. The celebration for tomorrow, and all that. It's tradition."

It felt strange for me not to know about these things. I had spent my time reading and researching everything from splinter-bombs to the history of Lyric Prime. But I had neglected current events. And Ari, when he was with me, had other things he wanted to do than talk to me about palace procedure or celebrations of light. I was not about to complain.

We all boarded the hover-pad with its central benches and red velvet drapes about the handrails. The hover took us effortlessly up and over the slowly paling moonscape. The ashy dirt unfolded below us like undulating, gray light with clots and eddies of darker shadows. In the near-distance, the base glowed. The black tarmac was dotted with flame-orange lights on the ground and above it, suspended as if on invisible poles, hanging fires to mark the way for incoming ships.

Ari stood next to me, hair blown lightly back from the motion of the craft, brown eyes flashing. His lips pressed tightly together when he looked at me, holding back a grin. From this response, among others over the past weeks, I did not have to guess or speculate to confirm he was shy to show affection in public. But the light in his eyes danced when his gaze met mine.

The hover stilled at the edge of the landing field. Everyone began to disembark, though nothing yet could be seen.

But before I reached the step, the sky cracked purple-blue-green like a bruise. Through the radiating hues of that dark spectrum emerged three golden lights following along the firmament as if in a linked arc.

My gaze followed the lights as I stood at the edge of the platform. The closer they came, they took on shapes. One was a disk with blue and pink lighting along the rim. Another seemed to have stretched wings beneath the head of a swan. The third came on like a curved sword, a scimitar, tumbling end to end.

Even in the vids I viewed throughout my life I had never seen anything like this. My pulse beat in my throat as I watched the scimitar ship approach so fast it seemed it would crash. It froze abruptly a few yards from touchdown, then slowly sank, its curved ends pointing upward as the base of the hull met the ground. The swan and disk did the same, seconds after their leader, but a lot more graceful.

I wondered if daredevil was a required trait to apply to pilot the scimitar starships.

They were all works of art.

Doors opened. Gangplanks lowered. People emerged in bright and shining colors.

Ari called my name.

I looked down. I was the last one still standing on the platform, staring at the spectacle, hypnotized. He waved me over to him as I descended the stairs and I found myself standing between him and the king as strangers of all ages and sizes and genders approached, bowing greetings and accepting Kean's embraces. Kean liked touch. That was his way. He hugged each and every regent, showing no favoritism, and introduced them to his son and then to me, describing me as the "esteemed palace empath." So many names. So many moons. Dira of Wolfeye. Kranistipol of Darkquill. Chartoaz of Seedglow. Tiiga of Snoglobe. And five more that ran over me so quickly I forgot them immediately. No doubt every four-year old on every moon knew the names of all ten moons as well as their regents. But I still couldn't remember them unless prompted.

My homework had focused on other things like Firgone's gothic city Xia, and now destroyed Lyric Prime, and a certain cursed crown prince. At least the visitors all spoke the same dialect of Galactic Standard so I could understand them.

The regents were quite attentive to Ari, praising his health, amazed at his so-quick recovery. The tragedy of the ruling family as well as the entire culture of the Realm of the September Stars had been so severe that several stated they did not believe the stories of Prince Arulu's healing until seeing it with their own eyes. Arulu's plight had been that hopeless. And this culture did not seem to focus on media as any reliable bearer of good news. I couldn't blame them.

Surrounded by beautiful starships and hanging fires, I still half-believed I'd wake up back at the Onyx Temple, and all this part of some splendor of a dream.

Ari whispered in my ear, his warm breath feathering my short hair, "You like the ships?"

"They're amazing."

I shook more hands. Kean embraced more people.

Then we were off, back to the palace. I couldn't help but think I hadn't really been invited on this excursion, but it had all worked out well. Maybe being invited wasn't their way, for I was welcomed anywhere I managed to just show up.

One hover was not enough for all the people, so a second one was called and showed up within minutes.

Upon arrival, the guest-wing quickly filled to capacity with all the newcomers. Overflows ended up on other levels but no one complained because all accommodations of the palace were richly furnished.

I said to Ari as we were walking down one of the corridors, "I wish you'd told me about the Coming of the Light."

He shrugged prettily. "I know. I should have."

"Do we do presents or anything like that?"

"You don't have to."

Which translated to my mind as "yes". And for a moment I was furious with him. This was a big deal. The fury faded as soon as it came, and I said, "Well, you and your father have given me so much. Maybe I can find something for you."

"I have everything I could ever need."

"Something you don't need, then."

He took a deep breath, as if exasperated, and made a face. I smacked him lightly on the shoulder for that look. To my delight, he chuckled. "Hey, what was that for?"

"Everything," I replied.

He shook back his long hair and traipsed on ahead of me as if to hide his feelings. But I knew what would happen when we got back to the privacy of our rooms. He would push me toward the bed as he kissed me, shy or playful or earnest, depending on his mood. Later, he would hold onto me all night as tightly as he could, even through the nightmares he didn't remember in the morning.

4.

With all the new visitors, major meals, like dinner, had been moved to the big banquet hall on one of the palace's uppermost floors. I had never seen this vast room before. It was Coming of the Light Eve.

When I entered the big hall I immediately felt lost. Larger, even, than the throne room, it held an endless array of fancy tables, shining glassware, and silver-gold and scarlet decoration. Giant dragons with finned tails and bird wings were carved into the marble walls on two sides of the room. Some of the dragons flew free in their marble skies. Some were tangled together, fangs exposed and fire cascading along the more amber colored marble sections. Fighting dragons so big and so realistic that if they came to life for even a second, their tails swiping outward, they'd dash all the fine tables to the floor.

I knew Ari had arrived before me, and I looked for him through the throngs of people and tables. A dash of red stood out. A dark head bent. Long hair reflecting the light in waves of green and gold.

I started to make my way to him when I was stopped by three strangers, delegates by the look of their attire though it was hard to tell; everyone from the Realm of the September Stars dressed well. Or courtiers. A term my brain came up with in the dialect of these people that I'd learned/downloaded.

Two men and one woman stood before me. The two men wore gray and black, more subdued than I was used to from the residents of Firgone, and yet elegant and shining. The woman wore her dark hair pulled up into half-braids and twists. She had on shimmering dark blue trousers and a white coat dotted with a hundred silver studs, each one projecting a tiny, dull spike. All three wore a lot of bracelets and rings.

One of the men said, "You're the healer."

"Yes. Tahir." I politely introduced myself.

They made no move to touch me, but stood back almost rudely appraising me.

The woman said, "You healed the prince."

"Yes."

"How amazing. The king tried so many times, with so many people, and always failed."

I did not like her tone which was part disapproving and part suspicious. But lack of trust was something, as an empath, I was used to. "My gift is unique," I replied. I refused to say more for fear it might be seen as bragging. That wasn't my way.

"Yes, so I've heard," she said.

The third man was ominously silent. He never took his eyes off me.

"So how does it work?" she asked boldly.

Something prickled along my spine, a sense like being backed into a corner. Remaining as amicable as I could, I generalized. "I take the disease into myself. My gift dissipates it."

"Impressive," said the man who'd first spoken. "You'd be worth your weight in blue diamonds to the gutter worlds where medical facilities are in short supply."

The woman said to him, without taking her eyes off me, "Didn't you hear, Valari, he's actually from one of those worlds." Then she said a word my knowledge of their language did not translate. "Kalalo."

Ignoring her, he said, "Really?" His perfectly shaped eyebrows, shaved at the ends, rose at me. "Which world?"

I was not sure how to behave. I wanted to look away. But something inside me held his gaze. I remained silent.

"Well?" he prompted.

The woman said, "Maybe he doesn't like to say."

The man had gray eyes flecked with gold. They were hard and dull, as if the light of the room never reached them.

"Alluria," I said.

His smile came on fast, but never unlocked his frozen face. "Ah, I've heard of it. Poverty levels at fifty percent. A shame with so much galactic wealth that goes to waste. Or is embezzled. Or pillaged."

If that was a reference to Lyric Prime's tragedy, it was a cold one. But then I realized these people would not come easily to trust. For the past twenty years they had lived behind a shield. They did not play well with others anymore. Even Arulu had been difficult, for many reasons. And his mother was still cold toward me.

Just then Ari walked up and the three strangers bowed to him, backing a step.

The woman said, congenially, "You look well, Prince Arulu."

"Thank you," he said with a half-smile.

"My name is Alir, and this is Valari and Rysen. We are from the Darkquill contingent."

"Nice to meet you. Dinner is about to start." Ari, not one for social graces, turned abruptly. To me, he repeated, softer, "Dinner is about to be served. We need to take our seats." He touched the top of my hand with his own.

I saw the others drop their gazes to observe this. Their faces tightened. On instinct, I pulled my hand back but not before I saw Valari chuckle, whispering, "Kalalo, really? That's low even for you, Alir. He seems to appeal to the prince's tastes."

"It seems," she said under her breath.

I turned away, my skin tingling from embarrassment and disgust, and walked behind Ari toward the royal table which stood out. He had been oblivious to the attitudes of the three courtiers. It was probably for the best.

The royal table was decked out in a violet drape with gold edging, and a quartz crystal fountain of purple wine chattered at its center.

All the colors, the hot aromas of meat and fine soups and fluffy cakes, the luxuries of refined metal utensils, china cups and plates, colored glass decanters and goblets, overwhelmed me. My vision blurred.

I had the sharp and sudden reminder I was an alien here and for a moment longed for the quieter, more sedate rooms at the Temple, the plain wood tables, the stone cups and plates, and the soft-spoken banter of the other acolytes, my foster brothers and sisters.

The colors of the table mixed in my gaze; for a moment I was displaced.

Ari said, "Tahir, what are you looking at?"

I realized I was staring at the fountain. But not seeing it. The trickle of the wine made a hushed splashing amid all the other noise.

"Tahir?"

I blinked.

Ari said, "Are you all right?"

"Yes."

"Here's your seat." He pulled out my chair for me, which made feel even more self-conscious as I noticed more and more surreptitious glances our way. Ari seemed oblivious.

I sat and turned to him. "What does kalalo mean?"

He frowned intensely. "Nothing good. Why? Where did you hear it?"

Not content with that answer, I said again, "What does it mean?"

"A colloquialism. Slang. Not really used in polite company, like fuck."

I asked a third time. "What does it mean?"

Ari sighed. "Well, it's like the shit that's been in the cesspool the longest, or something that no longer belongs. Also enemy, or outsider, of the rudest sort."

"Thank you." Now I scanned the room, looking for that trio, but I never spotted the Darkwell contingent again throughout the rest of the dinner.

*

Much later in the night, when we were in bed, Ari said, "You seem distracted." He kissed the edge of my jaw, a feathery, dry touch. A sweetness in the gesture that warmed my eyes.

A blue sheet covered my groin and part of my hip. Ari lay on his side, his upper body leaning over me, stark naked. His breath smelled of wine, and a little of the sugared cookies we'd had after dinner. His body gave off a fresh, slightly salty fragrance that always made my blood rush in my veins.

Here I was, with the most beautiful of lovers, and I stupidly kept thinking of those three delegates. The foremost thought I couldn't rid myself of: *You are not wanted here.*

I had prepared for disapproval. Rejection. Mistrust. But this, after weeks of feeling like I was fitting in better every day, threw me right out of my complacency.

Ari said softly, "Tahir?"

I smiled up at him, my breath catching. "It's nothing. Just feeling a little homesick tonight. No reason."

His mouth was down-turned, his eyes shadowed and deep. He ran his free hand through my short, white hair, over the side of my face, slowing to caress my cheek. The warmth of that hand slid down to my neck, petting, then to my chest.

He said, "I've wondered that you might like to see your home again."

"Really? You've wondered that?"

"Of course." Then his face broke open with the biggest smile I'd ever seen on him. "We have the best starships in the galaxy, you know. Its not like it's out of reach."

But the barrier-net was in place. People didn't just come and go in and out of the Realm as they pleased.

My eyes heated. "I know." But what I hadn't known was that he had thought of my feelings in that vein. Ari was socially backward in a few ways, still flighty with sudden and fleeting emotions. He gave me himself, yes, and he was educated, but he didn't regularly give voice to long thoughts, and spoke poetically only in bed. He listened to me when I talked. His comments, though, were often one syllable.

Now he surprised me when he asked, "Does this have anything to do with that word you asked me about at dinner?"

I didn't want to lie, so I said nothing.

He leaned in and rested his head next to mine on the pillow, facing my cheek. "It seems like it would be hard, leaving everything you've ever known," he said. "But you always seem fine, very sure of yourself. It's hard to think you might—" He stopped speaking, hand still rubbing circles on my chest.

"Might what? Have feelings?" I asked.

He pushed himself closer, chin against my neck, and said into my ear, "That's not what I meant."

I said nothing.

He added, "You're a hero here. My father gave you a title. Palace Healer. You're amazing. Really amazing." He lifted his head to look at me but we were too close. All I could see was a haze of skin, and feel his breath. He touched his forehead to mine. "You're the most amazing person I've ever met."

I let out a short laugh. "Right now, in this position, you'd say anything."

"No." But I felt him smile as his lips touched the corner of my mouth. "I mean it. You're brave and smart, and all that." He kissed me. Dry and gentle. Reverent. "You're breathtaking."

I wrapped one arm loosely about him.

He leaned into another kiss, pulled back and said, "What can I do to prove it to you? That you are these things? At least, to me."

Over his head I saw the deep white ceiling, slightly curved, and below that the window, not so dark anymore as Firgone was about to experience its once-a-year dawn. The night had turned grayer, and in just a few hours the sun would come up to stay. The dome would darken to keep the shade, but the light would make everything brand new. Just as I was getting used to the shadow-backed twilight, and the heaping mass of darkness that was Xia. That city, too, would transform like the moonscape. Would it be beautiful or ugly?

Still confused at my distractedness, Ari said, "Did I ever say that word to you that you asked me about, like maybe when we first met when I was so out of it? When I was angry?"

"What word?"

"Kalalo."

"No. You didn't." I ran my hand up his back and knotted my fingers in his hair. "You never said that word."

"Then why--?"

"Shh." I pushed at the back of his head, tugging a little at the hair, and forced his lips against mine. When I thought about how much I loved him, and in so short of a time, I felt both fierce and afraid. A fluttery fear scraped along the insides of my ribs. My stomach muscles tensed as if anxious for a confrontation.

Everything about this situation I now found myself in made me vulnerable, pondering, happy and sad, and strongly aroused. This man, who was really no younger than I, but seemed so, drew me like nothing I'd ever known.

I kept thinking it was my empathy doing this to me, blowing everything out of proportion. But Ari himself had a kind of forbearance and innocence and darkness all rolled together that was irresistible.

"Come here," I said huskily, and pulled him on top of me.

For a long time we kissed. He rubbed against me over the sheet, not rushing for once, just letting things play out. That made me smile because he was growing up so quickly, maturing before my eyes from pain-filled, spiteful, bitter man-child to a more patient, impeccable adult. Still grief-touched, yes, but searching for other ways to define himself.

I lay kissing him for long moments, thinking, contemplating, assessing my body before making an intimate decision.

"Ari, just a second." I pushed him up a bit, then twisted, reaching over the side of the bed where we kept the towel and some other things we sometimes used.

He fell to the side, his weight solid against me. Heated. The air was cool and dry around us.

I straightened up, holding a small vial of oil.

We sometimes used it to get slicker grips, friction that wasn't harsh or coarse.

I sat up and poured some into my hand, then turned, pushing him into the bed sheets and reaching for his erection, spreading that smooth richness all over his groin.

He moaned, closing his eyes, turning his head to one side and into the gilt pillow.

When I moved to straddle him, his eyelids flew open. He looked me up and down and I knew what he saw. My nude body above him, the skin smooth, not quite as hairless as he, with a trail of pale hair leading down to a bigger patch of silver-blond tangles that framed my genitals. I wanted him. That would be apparent. But now I wanted him a little more than he might be used to.

I poured another liberal amount of oil into my cupped hand and curved my arm behind me, rubbing and pressing the oil into the opening to my body, moving slightly back and forth as I did so.

He blinked, eyes wide. I saw he still wasn't sure what I was doing.

I opened myself, already wanting that, knowing what it would feel like so there was no shock for me. No indecision. It made the preparation easier, quicker.

"Tahir—" Ari began.

"Shh. I want to feel you deeper." I put the cool vial aside, leaning over him with one hand on either side of his shoulders. I kissed him deeply, rubbing my backside against him, slick against slick. "Just move with me," I whispered against his cheek.

We had never done this before and there was no way we were going to talk about it. So I was just going to do it.

I reached between my legs and grasped him. He was hard like stone. That alone made me supremely satisfied, just seeing him like that with me. I held him firmly, then teased myself with the head.

Ari's hands came up as if to grab at me, but he was too fascinated to do more, too aroused to question. His palms lay against my thighs. He started to breathe a little harder before I'd even done a thing. But of course he knew what was coming. He was thirty. He lived in a bisexual society. He knew what people did even if he didn't do those things himself.

Finally, I pushed the tip into me and slowly began to lower myself upon him.

He gasped, then held his breath as he watched my face, then his gaze moved lower, eyes huge.

My body opened fairly easily to him, not because I'd done this before (that had been so long ago anyway), but because I wanted him. Because I loved him. Gradually, he filled me, the

32

sensation like liquid silk but also a lovely hard intrusion. Lovely. Different. Intriguing. I moved slightly to see if I could stimulate myself inside, that special spot I'd learned about with Nik.

When his organ touched there, a solid pressure, my body gave a little shiver. Did he know about that? Did he know what this was doing to me?

I watched his face. Concern sharpened his features but soon lust gracefully softened them, and that was when I saw he couldn't help but trust me. A part of him wanted this, but he hadn't known until now.

When I felt my buttocks become flush with his hips, I took a breath. He took a breath.

I bent at the waist and put both hands on his chest. His hands fell away from my thighs. I felt fine, just stretched tight. Stretched thin. But not too thin. I looked into his rapt, and maybe a little scared, face and said, "You don't have to do anything. But if you want to thrust, you can."

At my words, his eyes fell shut. His mouth fell slightly open. I rocked myself against him and within I could feel the fires begin, the flames that licked at the knot of desire in my gut starting to undo all my tension. Gone was the stress of the before-dinner conversation. Gone that homesick feeling. Gone an emptiness that had resided in me my whole life.

The lube worked to make everything fluid, gliding, comforting, and arousal flared along my whole body, my skin fevered and sensitive, my erection aching. In this position, I could control how he slipped against the gland inside me, stimulating me even more.

Ari gasped. His hands tore at the sheets and his eyes flew open, closed, open again. He cried out. "Tahir!"

I felt him move under me. His hips rose to meet my moves. He was close. This wasn't going to last, but first times never did.

We moved together, surprisingly graceful, and much of my pleasure came from seeing him go crazy beneath me, knowing that I could clench and milk him to an ecstasy like no other, and that my own climax was rising with total abandon.

His hands uncurled from the sheets and grabbed my hips, holding me as I rode him. One hand strayed and grabbed my backside, pulling on the soft flesh there, and it felt like I was opening even further as he pushed up and I pushed down. His voice made a small, clenched cry. On that brink, he had no breath left, nothing.

I squeezed my internal muscles hard and looked into his face. Soft. Radiant. The whimper that began in the back of his throat made his Adam's apple quiver, and the way he looked so desperately pleading and beautiful nearly destroyed me. In that moment all galaxies and all worlds condensed to the two of us, and his fingernails dug into my skin. He shuddered. His muscles rippled in the pre-dawn light like liquid amber. He came.

I moved to follow him, but couldn't quite make it. As if he read my mind, one of his hands closed over me, stroking, tightening; then I came, too, cracked open from within. Obliterated.

I crashed against Ari's body heavily, feeling him slip out of me but still hard against my body. His arms came around me. I put my head against the side of his neck and bit the skin there, more teasing than hurting, as I labored to catch my breath. His own gasps burned against my shoulder.

I stretched my legs out and Ari's legs twined with mine. We rolled to our sides and clutched each other, wordless, for many minutes. I think I dozed off because the next thing I knew Ari was pulling a blanket over us both and saying softly, "Here," as he straightened his pillow beneath both our heads. A hand carded my hair. Lips brushed my forehead. Ari, usually the one so desperate to be held, held me now as I faded back to sleep.

5.

Part of the giant banquet hall had been transformed into a glittering dance space. Strange, live music played from an alcove, a combination of what sounded like flutes, bumpy sticks rubbing together, and the clanging of large pieces of falling metal. The musicians were hidden by a dark, velvet curtain, so I couldn't really see what was making all that noise.

This culture had a hand-up on the arts, but I wasn't sure music was included in that. It was thunderous and hurt my ears.

Still, people managed to dance to it, and the dance floor was already writhing with brightly-colored humans. Even more decorations had been added to the walls and ceiling. Before things had been tasteful, now they bordered on gaudy. The beautiful wall-sculpted dragons had been interrupted (and some totally covered) by embroidered drapes and thick, bristly-gilt garlands.

By every place setting sat brightly covered boxes. Gifts.

My stomach flipped. I had brought nothing for the king. And Ari, who couldn't care less about this holiday, could not be counted on to tell me what I should or should not do as expected by cultural decorum. Also, I had forgotten to ask.

He had come into the hall with me, but was immediately waylaid by strangers who surrounded him, gabbing incoherently. I was pushed aside, and getting used to it. It didn't really bother me. I wasn't their prince. I was, actually, more a hired hand. And glad enough to be so.

The festivities were all-out. Piles of food on golden plates. Fountains of wine at every table. Ribbons and presents and laughing, happy people. Survivors. The sun would rise. The dawn would come. They threw a party for it as if all the past, the bad and the dark, were forgotten. I admired them for it. Their art. Their ways. I could almost merge into it myself and forget the past. Almost.

I was still out of place, not yet fully absorbed by the intricate beauty and their flowering dialect of Galactic, and the way that everything fitted effortlessly. My job, though impressive to others, was not in demand. Though I had Ari, I still felt alone. He had a destiny. I was his lover but it ended there. Life was bigger for him than it was for me right now.

I went to one of the purple fountains and filled a crystal goblet to the brim. I did not sip slowly. The wine warmed me, sweet and cloying, and I drained the glass, going for a second helping.

Just to take the edge off the nerves, I told myself.

I turned toward where I had left Ari. I couldn't see him, the crowd was too thick. People wanting to check for themselves that he was back, he was healed, he was their crown prince. They wanted to touch him to confirm it, though I knew he wouldn't like that, hands on him, shaking palm to palm, hugging. But he would withstand it. He was already maturing rapidly into the man he should have become ten years ago.

I could not help but think his hunger, after being alone within himself for so long, warmed to me and me alone because I was there when no one else was. Because I was the healer. Convenient. But then I remembered how he'd searched for me in Xia. How he'd pushed me against that wall and held me in a grip of such zealousness as he kissed me. And every night thereafter, well, it had become a little more than "just convenient".

I traced my fingers along the silken table cloths as I walked along the edge of a chairless buffet, nails catching on appliqués of little scenes, gardens under night skies, suns and moons, and starships shaped like birds, sailboats, ribboned bows. All these designs billowed out from the tables in skirts. Gorgeous and detailed. My hand moved over cool cutlery laid out. And stack after stack of gold and silver plates. Covered and uncovered dishes were everywhere. No one had begun to eat yet, because everyone waited for the king. The hot dishes would come later after the king sat.

I looked up and around me. I still had so much to learn.

Across the hall the dancers moved. The music coughed and clanged. Bright faces and lots of smiles. And then I saw them. The three. Together at the other end of the table. They glanced away when I looked up. But they'd no doubt been watching me.

The delegates of the Darkquill contingent from last night. *Kalalo.* You are not wanted.

The king was talking animatedly in one corner. Winter, the queen, was nearby with her friends. Ari was surrounded, probably hiding his mortification, but I couldn't get to him through that crowd to lend support. I stood alone.

The three glanced around again. The woman met my eyes. I swallowed hard but did not look away.

Then I decided to do something bold. I raised my glass to her, then upended it and drained it.

A soft, slow buzz entered my head.

I turned away and as I did, the king was coming up behind me. His arm went warmly around my shoulders. Kean. So extraordinarily friendly. "Tahir. My personal hero," he greeted me. I had had two glasses of wine combined with too many maudlin thoughts so I could not control the flush that came rapidly over my face.

Kean was not by himself, always surrounded, followed by his entourage as well, but in that moment I felt he was there only for me, that he and I were strangely alone. "Come," he said. "I have gifts for you, diye."

The word came into my head as unfamiliar until my language training supplied it from memory. Foster-son. And the "e" on the end, when pronounced, meant favored. Kean had pronounced it.

Kean's arm was around my shoulders, his fingers closed strongly against my upper arm, wrinkling the green satins of my coat. He steered me to the main dais, raised, where Winter and Ari would sit with him. And myself. Always. Though it embarrassed me. I had not one drop of royal blood within me.

And Ari and I were certainly not married.

He took a gift from a pile on the table and handed it to me, making a motion that I should open it.

Now more people were watching. I put my wine goblet down and set about unknotting the elaborate silk ribbon. I pulled off the lid and lifted out a gold sun, a brooch as big as my fist but flattened, and worked with intricate, abstract designs of spirals and curves and moons.

I looked up.

Ari had come to the far end of the table within view.

The king said, "It is the royal healing crest. From—before."

The noise of the room still echoed, but softened. The surrounding group was completely silent, as if everyone were holding their breaths.

"Before" with this crowd always meant pre-destruction of Lyric Prime. *Before* twenty years and some odd months ago.

I may have healed the prince, but I was not one of these people. Not an artisan. Not a politician. Not a survivor. I'd simply been born with a gift. I did not deserve this. But I bowed to the king and stated, "I am honored."

A hint of a smile quavered against Ari's sensual lips.

But I was afraid. Any talk about before the splinter-bomb, when these people were at the prime of their culture, their inventions and their art, might cast a grisly shadow over celebratory events.

But Kean said, "You wear it, traditionally, with a cloak or a high-necked blouse. It fastens at the throat. But on your lovely jacket, to the right and above the breastbone will work." He reached for my gift only to deftly pin it upon me before I could utter one word.

There was applause, but not everyone clapped, and I kicked myself for feeling more mortified than honored. For this was the king, and not only had he called me his favored foster son, he'd given me both a title and now a crest. I couldn't be more welcomed than this. But I was so woefully ignorant still, of pomp and circumstance, of the ways political winds blew here, of the general mood of the crowd. I had not had enough time to study it all. Ten moons meant ten worlds with ten different populations. Lyric Prime had been the homeworld within a system of populated moons, with even more for me to learn about. Thousands of years had gone by since humans from old-Earth had seeded this sector.

But I made myself smile. I embraced the king. I quirked an eyebrow at Ari and people seemed to like that.

The king then settled at his seat, which was the sign for the dancers to come from the dance, the music to draw back to more sedate, dulcet tones, and people to gather round all the lavish tables and begin the first course of the feast to celebrate the Coming of the Light.

I took more wine. My plate gleamed up at me, blinding. Ari's heat radiated toward me, his seat close, his thigh only inches from mine.

Ari leaned toward me and whispered quickly into my ear, "You look a little green."

I took up my wine glass and toasted him. "Just need more wine," I replied a little too loud.

He took up his glass and drank with me.

My thoughts buzzed. The food looked fuzzy but still appetizing. I ate small bites, as the wine, the most important part of the meal, churned through my veins.

Everything about the room flashed and shimmered and glared. So many lights. All the gilt. Even the centerpieces of the tables, leaf-crowns surrounding flared glass containing wickless flame, were plated with metallic colorings. Enough to hurt the eyes.

The king commented to me often, things I immediately forgot, but I nodded anyway. Ari was quieter, as usual, but his body looked tense with delight despite his confession he hated this holiday. He seemed to be absorbing the festive atmosphere, and he ate hungrily, which pleased me. He needed it. His ribs and spine still showed through his skin more than I, as a healer, liked to see. Through the eyes of a new lover, however, I saw him as not even the tiniest step away from perfect.

At the thought, my entire body heated. I sipped more wine.

The brooch was heavy against my breast, even through the thickness of the layered satins. It bumped. It branded. My skin started to sweat. I wanted to get up, move around. But dessert was still one course away and I didn't want to be rude.

I made myself take deep breaths.

Ari said to me, "An excess, I know. I'm stuffed."

I chuckled, trying to regain my equilibrium. I didn't think I would throw up, but I was feeling so hot. "Then you won't be offended if I pass on dessert?"

"No."

I wanted to take my jacket off. But the brooch. The formal quality of the meal. I didn't dare.

Protocols. I tried to wrangle them in my foggy brain.

Of course. Bodily functions were always excused. I could say I needed the lavatory. Get up. Walk a little. Get some air. I needed to put the roiling in my belly at ease, clear my head.

I felt bombarded by everything, the holiday that came without warning, the king's gift, the contingent from Darkquill. My love for Ari that stirred me to my deepest core with a delicate, luscious ache that all on its own made worlds spin.

My body chose this very moment to remember when he was inside me. I looked up at the flashy, scintillating banquet throngs. My face flared so hot I thought the whole room would see its flames.

I couldn't stay seated. I rose and turned to Kean. "It's all such a delight, but the facilities call." I tried to make the language formal, but nonchalant.

Ari hissed, a desperate plea. "Leaving me to the great battle ahead?"

"I'll be back." I forced a grin.

He nodded and waved me away.

So many people had gathered in the great hall; there was always someone coming or going. So I wasn't the only one.

As part of the royal table, I was allowed to make my way behind the festivities, instead of through the front doors, and down a more darkened hall flagged by much fewer garlands and curtains of deep green velvet.

The lavatory was not my destination, though. I'd drunk a lot, but it had dehydrated me. What I needed was to breathe away from too many people and too many colors and fragrances and the air tremoring with clinky alien music, and metal knives hitting metal plates, and never-ending melodious voices discussing nothing.

The crest bent the satins of my coat downward on the right. Heavy enough to tear if I caught it on a doorframe or a chair. I wanted it off. But I didn't touch it. Drops of sweat rolled down my back like hot lava. Burning. I managed to walk upright, but my head swam as if air had been forbidden to me, though I breathed fine.

Well, I thought, I am a ridiculous mess.

I wanted to run. Or maybe yell. Two things that should have been minor but weren't. The three from Darkquill. The word *Kalalo*. The equation ended thus: I could not hope for any emotional security on an alien moon where some saw me as an intruder.

I had come from a planet where I had purpose, and moved to a place where I had none. Pathetic.

But when I thought of Ari, a strength welled inside of me, along with that charming ache for him. Simply, I wanted him with me. And damn it, I would fight for that.

I should not abandon the celebration, but I only wanted to walk, now, then go back to our rooms. Ari could chime me through the necklace if he needed me.

I moved toward the outer corridor, avoiding the restrooms entirely. I came through a curtain to an alcove that smelled like dust, and pushed the button to open the door there. I expected to see escorts lingering up and down the hallway. But there was no one. It seemed I'd eluded even my own, the faithful Sullen and Taridia.

The top level of the palace was comprised mostly of the banquet hall. The corridors were curved and led to steps or hover platforms. I decided I would take the steps. Distantly, I heard the echoes of the party, the celebrants laughing, glasses tinkling. It was a night when worries were laid aside, and revelry replaced concern.

The air was cool and dry. The moonscape appeared beyond the thick, carven banister of the stairway. Under the dome the land was paler now, ashen when before it had been coal. Dawn was coming.

Despite my dizziness, I was steady enough. *Four flights*, I told myself, looking at the massive spiral staircase so beautifully wrought of moonstone and black rock, veined with gold. *Four flights down and down until you clear your head.*

Something shifted behind me, cloth on cloth, faint soft shoe against a stone, cold floor.

I turned, expecting maybe Sullen had found me, ever vigilant. Instead I saw a dark, hooded figure, shimmering in black velvet, and behind him two more. He came at me so fast I didn't realize I had been hit until I crashed against the base of the banister, my head hitting the wall.

I had no time to think about what was happening before more blows came, and my body was smacked back against the stone of the floor, my head ringing. Something kicked my side, my back. Another kick came in front, right between my legs.

I let out a moan with a great push of air. Hands grabbed my coat and tore. Then I realized they were taking the crest.

A voice hissed, "This does not belong to you!" I could see only glimpses of dark fists and boots, and the back wall of the gold-lit corridor, and then I heard the coat's satin tear, and saw the gold glint of the crest fly up and over my head. The brooch arched through the air and over the banister, disappearing into the night. It was such a long way down, I knew I'd never hear it reach the ground of the bottom floor.

My jacket hung at my elbows. More fists punched me in the stomach, chest and thigh. They grabbed at the jacket until, ripping, it was flung aside.

From somewhere came a shout and the three assailants leaped down the stairs on swift legs, never uttering another word. They were gone as quickly as they'd come.

People came running. Sullen was there, his arm under my neck, and calling my name. Taridia was behind him. And then others. All a blur.

I assessed my body. No broken bones. Nothing serious. I was breathing. I was alive. "I'm okay." But my throat ached when my voice came out. I was shaking.

I pushed Sullen away and tried to stand. He ignored my shoves, and helped me, and suddenly Ari was there, taking his place. "What happened? What happened?"

Through all the aches and pains of the beating, all I could actually feel was a sudden flood of embarrassment. People were looking at me. I was still drunk and my clothes were torn.

I still managed to stand, with Ari's help on the right, Sullen on the left. Sullen said viciously, "He was attacked!"

"They went down that way." I pointed at the stairs.

Immediately, several people ran the way of the assailants, but they'd been smart, too smart to be caught. It was too late anyway.

I looked at my coat on the floor. "I'm okay," I said again, trying to give myself back some dignity. I pressed my lips tight when I saw my beautiful green and purple jacket reduced to a pile of expensive rags. "My coat's seen better times, though."

"Looks like they got the crest," Taridia said.

"The king should not have given it so publicly," someone said.

Taridia nodded. "People still have deep feelings about the past."

"Shut up," Sullen said. "No one had the right to do this."

I leaned down, wincing as my body felt pain shoot from my hip to my back, but I didn't straighten until I had the coat in my arms. "I liked this coat," I said, and some people laughed, thinking I was trying to calm the situation. But anger was all I felt.

Ari said, one hand at my elbow supporting me, "Luckily, it can be replaced."

But the crest was gone.

The king came a moment later, and I thought, *Please don't make a scene.* I lifted my chin. "I'm fine," I said to him, by way of greeting. But his eyes were dark, furious.

"Tahir, this does not happen in my palace. I am in grief over this!" He reached out to cup my jaw. "You need medical aid."

"I need to lie down, that's it. Just some minor bruising," I assured him.

But the king ordered it anyway. Then he said to Ari, "Take him to lie down. I'll deal with the rest. I'll have the doctor sent to your rooms."

A hover platform was brought so I wouldn't have to walk. I had wanted to walk, damn it. But I didn't protest as they got me onto it, still clutching my ruined coat.

Ari went with me even though I told him he should go back to the party with Kean.

He said, "You're crazy if you think I'm leaving you."

"Tonight's a big deal, and you need to be seen. A lot of people traveled very far."

"I'll see them tomorrow."

I had wanted to be alone. Now I had more attention than ever. The shock of the attack made me angry. Rightly so, but I was so flustered I didn't trust myself not to yell at the wrong people. I didn't want medical attention. I didn't want the people following the hover-craft to our rooms. I didn't even want Ari there in that moment because I always worried about him being upset too much, and in this moment I didn't have the strength to deal with him.

My only winning move was to shut my mouth and look down at my ruined coat. I concentrated on breathing evenly. My teeth trapped my lower lip and even though I was hurting throughout my body, I bit down to feel that pain instead of everything else.

My mixed thoughts and feelings tried to overwhelm me. Fury. Shock. The almost irrational feeling that I was so out of my element, displaced, that I wanted to escape, hide. I knew I would calm down, but in the moment I couldn't see or think clearly at all.

My adrenalin had taken quick care of the muddled feeling of the wine, but this feeling of loss was different, deeper, too real.

Give me more wine, I thought, *and I'll be fine.*

Ari helped me from the hover-craft and to the door. I was grateful when he blocked anyone else from touching me.

6.

The door opened. I said softly to Ari, as we crossed the threshold, "Don't let anyone else in."

He turned and shut the door manually with the switch. "I'll just let the doctor in when she comes."

"No!" I pulled away from him and went to the bed, sitting. I placed my coat in my lap and just stared.

Ari came over and stood in front of me, staring.

"I'm fine," I said without looking up. "Please don't stare at me."

"I don't know what to do," Ari finally confessed.

"I told you to go back to the party."

"That is not an option," he replied, and now his voice came on tougher, when before he had been unsure, and possibly in as much shock as I.

I sighed loudly.

He said, "My father will want a full report."

"I know that," I said through gritted teeth. "I will give him one tomorrow."

Softer, "I know. Tahir." He reached for my coat. "Please lie down." He took the pile of green and purple satins from my arms and set it aside.

My breath caught in my throat to see that coat so damaged.

I finally lay stiffly back on the spread amid the throng of pillows. I looked toward the graying window, felt his weight next to me as he sat on the edge of the bed.

"Tahir," voice more uncertain now. "I'm sorry."

"You didn't do anything to be sorry for," I replied.

As I lay there, my body felt strangely light, as if all the air had been let out of it. My muscles felt as if they had suddenly become soft, liquid. The adrenalin that had been pumping through my system still raced through me, but less now, and I was starting to feel exhausted.

Ari said softly, as if having trouble gathering the words, "When I was at my worst, after I got a dose of the meds I would go into the hot shower or bath and it helped. Do you want that?"

"I don't think I can move that far right now."

"I'll help you."

I was in the hands of a barely healed man, but a loving one, at least. "Go ahead and start the water running. But if I'm asleep when you come back, don't wake me."

He didn't say anything more. After a moment, he got up. I didn't want to think this way, but it was blissful to finally be alone. I let my eyelids close, and my head swam. I saw blue and orange lights in my after-vision, then I was sinking.

Later, soft hands moved over my shoulders and around me.

I surfaced just enough to remember to say, "I told you not to wake me."

Without a word, Ari lifted my upper body against him and slid my legs off the edge of the mattress. He got me to my feet and guided me. I let him because a part of me realized hot water was probably going to feel like paradise after the night I'd had.

He sat me on the side of the giant tub—more like a pool—
that was one of the many luxuries afforded by bunking with
him. The water gently swirled and I saw masses of—

"Bubbles?" I asked.

"I think I put a little too much in," he mumbled, undoing
my shirt. He had it half off my shoulders before I realized he'd
moved to the trousers.

I pushed his hands away. "I can do that," I said.

"Sure." He went back to getting the shirt sleeves off my
arms, trapping them so I couldn't do anything about the pants.

"Tahir."

At the tone of his voice I looked up at him. He was gazing
at my ribs. I looked down. A large pink bruise was forming in a
circular pattern just below the bottom of the rib cage.

"I'll live," I said.

His hand on my shoulder pulled my upper body to one side
and he ran fingers down my back. "They kicked you."

"More bruises back there?" I asked.

"A few."

"It doesn't hurt to breathe." I took a big breath to prove it.

"Come on," he said, a little breathless now. "Let's get these
off." He took my soft, leather boots away, and proceeded to
divest me of my pants. I let him because I was just that tired,
and the water looked so good. All those bubbles. They smelled
of flowers.

I saw him grimace when he discovered yet another bruise
on my upper thigh. That one didn't hurt. I'd been kicked in the
groin, too, but I had twisted away on instinct, and that pain had
faded. No permanent damage, so that was good news. *All is
well*, I kept telling my battered brain.

On his knees now, he helped me slide into the warm,
swirling water. He'd taken off his own jacket, but the cuffs of
his sleeve got wet. Steam rose into my face and immediately
dampened my hair. I let out a groan. I couldn't help myself. The
encasing heat was as close to ecstasy as could be.

The tub was square, more like a deep pond, and made of rough-hewn, black marble, non-slippery. There were two gold faucets at each end, shaped like tiny, winged dragons. The wall had an inner alcove that housed brightly colored bottles of soaps, shampoos, and lotions. A pile of soft cloths, green, blue and gold, lay to one side on the shelf. From a nearby hook hung soft, round sponges, and a long back-brush. In the furthest corner, behind the bottles, sat a black plastic toy, a triangle ship with painted gold windows along the edge, and three hollow tubes at the rear. Some kind of alien fish sculpture was attached to the top, neat and small, giving the impression it was going to surf that ship through the stars. Or, rather, a galaxy of bubbles for a little boy who wanted toys in his bath.

I reached for it. Of course I'd seen it before, but I had never really looked at it. I'd just left it as the decoration it was. I held it up to my face, coating it with a foam of bubbles.

Ari said, "I have had that since I was five."

I looked up at him. He looked so worried. I gave him a sleepy smile and said, "I really am okay. I can't heal myself, but I can assess myself when injured or sick."

"It is weird," Ari said softly. "We now have a palace empath to heal us when needed, but who heals the healer when he gets sick?"

"Your medical technology is quite advanced."

"Oh yeah." He started to stand. "That reminds me. Will you be okay? I have to see to the doctor. I locked the door. If she's here she'll be waiting as my father ordered. I don't want her standing out there with the escorts all night."

I gritted my teeth. "Please don't let her in."

He turned at the door to look at me. I couldn't read his expression. Then he was gone.

I placed the toy starship on the surface of the swirling bubbled water. It floated, catching itself on the currents, making its slow way to the foot of the tub. I let it go and just lay back and tried to relax. The water frothed about me. It was the best medicine ever.

I think I dozed, because Ari startled me when he returned.

"It's all settled," he said. "The doctor's already left. I got some light pain pills for you, and an oil for the bruising. It'll help heal you fast."

"Thanks." My eye fell on the little toy bobbing its way along the edge of the tub as if looking for a path out, the fishie passenger hanging on for dear life.

It was a relief to know I wouldn't be poked and prodded by some surgeon I didn't need.

Ari sat on the edge of the tub again. I waved him away. "You'll get your pretty clothes wet."

He didn't move, but said, "I got an update. They haven't apprehended your attackers yet."

"They were efficient and smart. They're long gone."

"They're still on this moon. The base is closed down for the Coming of the Light."

"Well, anyway," I said, looking away, "they were just mad about the crest. That's all."

"They hurt you."

I blinked twice, then dunked myself to wash my hair. When I came up, water splashed but Ari did not move. I slicked my pale hair back with one hand and said, "You have to go back to the party. You have to be present. On a night like this—"

"Why are you trying to get rid of me?"

"I'm not. But you have duties now that you can't shirk." I failed to keep the irritation from my voice. Stress. I was immediately sorry.

But as I stood, the water sluicing off my body like a dozen crazy waterfalls, Ari stood, too, eyes sparkling, unable to keep from looking at my body head to toe. Normally, I would move closer to him and our arms would automatically go around each other. But I was still too shaken to think of it. He handed me a towel which I immediately wrapped myself in. Then he picked up my robe.

I stepped over the rim of the tub, quickly dried myself, and he held the robe open for me. It was long, white, and it completely enfolded me. The gesture of him helping me into my robe, just that, more than anything else good he'd done for me that night, nearly undid me. Ari had grown so much in the past month.

And his smile, the pink lips, the dark eyes, the long, unbraided hair, all just about perfect. His gray trousers were dotted with water. The red shirt looked less damp, but the folds of it at his shoulders and waist became rivulets of ruby where the material wrinkled as he moved. The top button was undone. His brown throat gleamed. He was so beautiful right then. I wanted to fall into his arms.

But disturbed as I was, I turned away from him and headed back to the bed.

As I sat, he showed me the things on the nightstand. "Oil, with cinnamon, for the bruising. It smells pretty good," he said, lifting it and taking a sniff. "And here are the pills." A small, orange bottle. "And water." The glass was emerald crystal, shimmering to the brim with cool, clear liquid.

Then he sat beside me, looking momentarily awkward. "What else can I do for you?"

"Nothing. I want to sleep."

He reached out and touched his palm to my wet hair, sliding his hand against it. "I'm so sorry," he said again.

I tried not to glare at him. They say healers make the worst patients. We wanted to do the work, but when it came to people fussing over us, we were awkward, shy. "You need to go back. To the party. The people. It will reassure them that everything is under control if you're there. They'll see that it's all well again. You'll tell them I'm fine, that there's no damage done."

He contemplated my words. "I don't—"

"I'll be here," I interrupted, "when you get back later."

A flicker of pain crossed his features.

"Please go. For me." I really did want to be alone.

He started to shake his head, turning to me, eyebrows narrowed. "Lie down."

50

I did as he told me. He lifted the top cover over me where I lay, robe and all. "I'll stay an hour at the party just to reassure everyone. That is all. Then I'll be back."

"Okay," I said. "Good."

Politics. He was learning. And, it seemed, so was I, albeit the hard way.

I turned to face the wall below the big window. After a long moment of silence, I heard his footsteps move across the tile floor, soft leather brushings, and then the whispering shush of the door opening and closing.

Heat welled in my eyes. I quickly closed them. Tight. Tighter.

My skin was still warmed from the bath, relaxed. The robe was too much. I sat up and threw it off, then settled back down.

My mind still buzzed, but with all that, and the havoc my body had been through, the sinking comfort of sleep finally found me.

*

I don't know how much time had passed when I woke to the feeling of a weight against my back and a hand coming over my waist to press against my belly.

Ari's skin was alive and aglow against me, a summery slide. My gut twisted with the beginnings of desire, but he settled quickly and lay still. I wanted to turn and speak to him, but I liked just lying there in the peace and comfort, listening to his breathing as it evened out, the air slow between his lips. The dregs of celebration had left a soft fragrance on him that filled the space in our bed, part wine, part salty sweat from the excitement (whether he wanted it or not) of being around a lot of people, and still a little tartness of hidden anxiety.

I leaned into him, pulling the covers tighter to my chest. My heart began to pound and I wasn't sure why. At that moment I knew only languorous security. But my body kept remembering those hard kicks, the fists, and falling against the banister wall and hard floor. There was a slight constriction in my breathing. It took a long time of concentration and meditative effort to calm myself again.

Finally, I sank into the heat of the bed and the comfort of Ari pressed up behind me, and went back to sleep.

7.

The new light came that morning. The cool, white dawn.

The sun rose slow, a pale sliver of a circle against the darkened horizon of the dome, an ashen eye just beginning to open. It would take weeks for it to rise and show its full form. But enough of it had come up to spill its silvery incandescence in rivulets across the moonscape.

I lay propped against the pillows, gazing out.

Ari had an arm thrown over his eyes, wincing. "I really prefer the dark," he muttered.

I had come to Firgone in the dark, and hadn't realized the change in season was so soon to arrive. I had fallen in love with the shadows and the weirdness of always feeling like it was half-past dusk. So far, it was all I had known.

"Me, too," I said.

Ari took his hand away from his face and leaned up on one elbow to look at me. "How are you feeling?"

"All right," I said, still looking out the window. Fleeting anxiety stirred my stomach.

He leaned back and grabbed the jar of oil the doctor had given me. "Let me put this on your back. You'll heal faster."

I rolled onto my side with my back to him and he gently rubbed the tincture onto my bruises. I loved the feel of his hands, careful but firm, warm and soothing.

"That feels good," I said softly.

Not replying directly to my compliment, he said, "I can get you an appointment with the palace masseuse. He's very good."

"No." I didn't want anyone else touching me. Especially strangers. Ari's soft touch was sufficient. He was all I wanted. No one else.

"I was so afraid for you last night," Ari said haltingly. "Still am. From now on, you must not go anywhere without the escorts."

"Is this how it is to be, then?"

I felt his forehead touch my upper back and nod.

"For how long?"

"Until the suspects are retrieved."

I turned onto my other side so we could see each other. "Ari, I don't hear gossip." I was so tired of feeling under-informed. "I don't see it on current events on the wave or anything like it. Anything about the king, or you, any news about the palace is always so short and business-like."

"On my father's orders."

"So there isn't free press here?" Where I was from, that had always been a right that was taken for granted.

"Is that what it's called when people gossip?" He gave a short laugh. "Then, no, we don't have it."

"So how do I learn about anything? How do I know what the prevailing moods are concerning you, the king, the palace, me—"

"I guess you talk to people."

I almost forgot I was asking questions of someone who did not pay attention to palace chatter or intrigue. He had had no interest or time or inclination for anything for so long. But now he was awake, aware, living in his father's domain, meeting his father every day.

I said, "Do you talk to people?"

"Not if I can help it."

I frowned.

"Lately, it can't be avoided," he added.

"And the prevailing mood about me is?"

"What do you mean?" He reached out and put his hand on my chin so he could look me in the eye. The new silver light gave his dark eyes a cooler, frost-edged gleam.

"Well, I'm an intruder, an interloper. And this culture is not a trusting one. For good reason."

"You healed me. They love you. Kean gave you the title of Palace Healer. That is an honor. People respect that."

"Ari, be honest for a minute. I'm an alien."

"We're both human."

"You know what I mean!" I didn't mean to sound angry.

Ari jerked back. "People love you for what you did for me."

Yes, but do people love you? Have they ever gotten to know you or see you in twenty-odd years? I didn't say that aloud.

Maybe the palace courtiers approved of me. They saw things first-hand. They knew how well I had pleased the king, healed their prince. But without real news or current event reporting, the rumors about their prince, and about me could be anything, not only here on Firgone, but on any of the other moons.

I had seen up close the looks on the faces of the three delegates from Darkquill. It was in their body language, their tone, their entire demeanor. *You are not wanted.*

I had thought about the fact that my hooded assailants were three people. Right after I was assaulted, I had thought of the three Darkquill visitors, their distaste, their insults. But I could not accuse them. My attackers were larger, all tall, and from what I could sense, all male. I never saw their faces.

There were now six people who disapproved of my presence, when two days ago there had been, to my knowledge, none. The prevailing mood was not as accepting as I'd been led to believe.

"Ari," I said, reaching up to touch his cheek. "I adore you, but sometimes you can be very naïve."

He said nothing, but his lips tightened.

"I understand why. You're still just waking from a nightmare. But let's not pretend otherwise."

54

He swallowed. "Are you saying I should have known of your danger in advance?"

"No."

"My father is doing all he can. He's taking care of it."

His father. The king. Yes. Ari was still only a shadow of that, of what he could or might become.

"When you are with your father, is there ever talk of me?" I asked. I had not told Ari what Kean had said to me about living together, and vat-grown children.

Ari shifted his knees against me. "Like what? I mean, he might occasionally say how grateful we should all be that we now have a gifted empath for our official Palace Healer."

"And the others in his entourage—do they respond?"

"No."

I wished Ari was more forthcoming. I wasn't sure how capable he was of observing and trusting his observations. He was still somewhat isolated in his mind, self-centered in the way that might make him miss things in others. He didn't easily trust, for he still had no friends other than me, and so he might fail to recognize outright duplicitous behaviors unless they were right in his face and aimed at him.

The downy pillows were soft about me. I leaned back against the wall, facing him. He was still sitting up as he had been when applying oil to my bruises. His legs were crossed now, a pillow on his lap. His hair was a tumble of storm clouds.

"What is the biggest ongoing discussion or decision that has happened since you started participating in meetings with the king?" I asked.

"There is a very major decision he and all the regents have participated in, both in person and long distance for weeks. A lot of research, a lot of talk."

"What? Are you allowed to say?"

He nodded. "To you I can say it. Because you have a title and you're part of this palace."

I waited. A flash of something internal crossed over his eyes, darkening them. I couldn't read him right then. I didn't know if it was fear or excitement or maybe he was just unsure.

He said, "Kean wants the barrier-net that hides the ten moons from the rest of the galaxy removed."

"What?" I couldn't believe what I was hearing. "Ari. That's huge. That's a really big deal."

He looked down and his dark lashes quivered. Softly, "I know."

"Obviously, a lot of people would be against that decision, right? It's barely been time for a generation to pass. And no one knows where the splinter-bomb attack came from and why."

"He says we're ready to open trade within the galaxy again. He's firm on that position."

There were a dozen thoughts that went immediately through my mind. Fear of change was one. Fear made people do desperate things. Fear made people attack strangers they thought might be usurping their territory, their crests, their crown prince.

I wasn't a politician, but I did have command of some common sense. Ari did not. His thinking was not designed in that way. At thirty, that might never change. He was better apt to remain a dreamer, fantasizing about the dead, or taking up his childhood hobby of drawing pretty pictures of starships on blank handscreens.

Yet, I had also noticed he was a quick thinker. A fast learner. He certainly wasn't stupid.

"Is there a lot of disagreement in the ranks?" I asked quietly.

"Some. It's all about negotiating. If this, then that." He paused. "Like people say, if you do this thing, then we want this other thing. Everyone has their hand out. Everyone wants something." He leaned forward into me.

I leaned also, meeting him halfway. Our foreheads touched. "What do they want?"

His shiver was almost imperceptible, but I saw it. I felt it. He sighed, then said very softly, "Weapons."

Ari. Victim of the worst weapon ever conceived. My fading bruises were nothing in comparison.

I put my arms around him and he came closer, moving his legs back so he could mold himself against me. He seemed at ease at first, but as I held him I noted his body had tensed. It was the first time I fully realized that my own attack was not about people angry over a crest. It was about fear. This palace and this moon was not the safe place I had thought it was.

8.

Firgone and its nine sister moons comprised all that was left of the colonized Lyric Prime system called the Realm of the September Stars. Before the splinter-bomb, and the alien destruction of Lyric Prime, its culture had known peace, both internally and externally, for over a thousand years. People felt safe. Weapons did not exist. Not real ones, anyway. There were antique scimitars and broadswords in existence, used mostly for decoration. They came from ancient times and cultures before terraforming and galactic colonization even existed.

The palace on Firgone was filled with them.

As for any kind of more advanced weapons, stun guns, lasers, plasma cannons or any other kind used in a star war, they manufactured none, and officially, as a governed people, owned none. They had no army, no warrior star fleet. They did not produce soldiers.

Their only defense against alien attack was technology they had quickly invented after their home world was destroyed.

The net.

It locked the galaxy out. Or seen another way, it imprisoned the people within it. The net made the ten moons and the sun they orbited invisible, and ships could not pass through without a special shield created by a technology known only to the people of the September Stars.

The fact that the people were now asking for weapons should the king decree the net to come down was unprecedented in their newer history. But then the fact that their realm had been attacked when they had been only a peace-loving people for so long was also unprecedented.

It stood to reason that culture would change to now reflect fear. Not only did the people want weapons, they wanted to employ trained mercenaries from other worlds to patrol their system of leftover moons.

My necklace chimed.

Want to go for a walk? the little screen read.

Okay.

Meet me at the foot.

"The foot" meant the base of the spiral stairs. It was the middle of the day. Not Ari's usual routine.

When I got to the bottom of the stairs, I saw him, stiff-backed and preoccupied, pacing in the ashen moon-dust before the palace pathways. I could tell he was having a bad day. He had two escorts who remained discreetly about twenty feet away.

My own escorts always flagged me now.

When he saw me he said, "Let's go toward the gardens."

He meant the hydroponics buildings, which housed beautiful atriums, aviaries and forest greenery.

He did not speak. Our walk was silent. After a few minutes, we approached a beautiful area just outside hydroponics, landscaped by moon rocks. In the center was a bench. He went to it and sat. I sat with him.

He leaned his elbows on his knees. "I wanted to tell you myself. It's almost final. The net *will* come down."

"When?"

"Weeks. At most. Kean thinks we're ready."

But one look at Ari and I could tell he was not ready. And he'd been doing so well these past weeks.

Ari said to me, "Personally, I think I'd rather stay imprisoned behind the net. It's less complicated. Why do we need the rest of the galaxy? Trade or anything? We have all we need here."

"Have you told Kean your opinion?" I asked.

"He never asks. He just tells."

I couldn't figure out why he would not state his piece to the king, but instead kept quiet. He was clearly upset.

We sat there on the bench squinting at the brightened, flat moonscape and distant rolling hills, still partially in shadow. The protective dome made it safe to stare directly at the slow-rising sun, an arch-shaped golden sliver burning just beyond the low, gray peaks.

It was not only the two of us sitting there, and that made things awkward. It seemed we could never be alone. The prince had his escorts; I had mine. They were with us all the time. The closest thing to soldiers among these people were the guards. They were trained in martial arts, but carried no weapons.

Ari, who was lovely today in green scarves and a gold, embroidered jacket, said so quiet I almost didn't hear him, "Tahir, I am not brave."

His words startled me. "You have endured more than anyone. And you're alive."

"Accident of circumstance," was his response.

"And your will. Don't forget, I've seen it." He knew what I meant. I had been inside his mind.

"I don't want to expose our worlds to the rest of the galaxy again. Aside from my first ten years of life, I've never known any other way."

"I know."

It was easy enough to understand why. The last time Ari had lived exposed to the galaxy had ended with the deaths of all his siblings, and terrifying injuries to himself. His viewpoint on this was completely rational.

Now he bowed his head, looking at his feet. His whisper came for my ears only. "When the net falls, I want to leave here, go away."

My heart nearly stopped. "You can't. You know that, right?"

He turned his head to the side to look at me. His eyes were dark pools, and I saw in them the twist of cold loss. He had been dutifully going with his father to every daily function and meeting, showing by his presence that the ruling family was still stable, that the Realm was no longer beset by a haunted prince. He came into my arms at night, showing me smiles I'd never seen from him before. Happy for those moments. Or so I thought.

He did not speak for a long moment.

"Ari, everyone feels that way sometimes."

"What if I told you I don't want this life and never did." His whispering was so soft I had to strain to listen. He did not want the escorts to hear him.

This was major, both politically, and personally. He could break the thinly-held civilization of the Realm, and he would break his father's heart. "Your timing for abdication would be destructive," I whispered back. I wanted to be on his side, the side of Ari, his feelings, what he wanted from this new life he'd been re-gifted. But as my thoughts worried the problem, I saw only the worst ramifications: downfall, civil unrest, and possible bloodshed. It wasn't my realm, my family, my culture. But of course now it was. I was here for the rest of my life. I had promised this. Vowed to the king.

"None of this is fair to me," Ari said. He wasn't whining. It was just a statement. Along with that still-lost look in his eyes.

"We need to talk in private."

He let out a short laugh. "My rooms are bugged."

"The bedroom, too?" I was appalled.

"Maybe not. I don't know for sure. I just trust no one."

I nodded. I wanted to take his hand but was afraid he would jerk away. We had not shown physical affection in front of the escorts, or anyone. So far. Even though our relationship was not a secret to the king, we still kept on our public faces.

I stood. "Let's just walk, then, okay?" I gestured to the building and its lush, inner gardens.

He slowly nodded. I held out my hand to pull him up from the bench. He took it. I squeezed it, holding onto it a moment longer than necessary after he was fully standing. He did not jerk away; my smile did not reflect the truth in my heart.

I realized in that moment, Ari and me—we had only just begun to know each other.

We walked through drapings of green, the foliage dripping, the air tropical, but not hot. All the layers of green filled my eyes, and the sounds of humming, and birds, and far-off cascading water. Everything smelled of rain and newness.

Ari seemed to visibly relax. This place took us far away from palace politics and concerns.

I did not know much about politics, ruling, princes or kings other than the fact they had human hearts with red human blood. But I did think that everyone, even the strongest among us, had doubts. Ari was facing a phase of that. Only a phase, I hoped. Because I had no idea how to advise him otherwise when he looked to me.

Then there was my contract with the king, which technically superseded Ari's will.

Ari blended beautifully with the gardens in his clothing of golds and greens. He flashed in a brilliance that spun my heart. To fall in love with someone first, and afterward slowly continue to learn about them gave me a lost feeling, but also a thrill. He could surprise me every day. Good or bad.

I hoped I did the same for him, the good part, at least.

Right now, as we walked, and I saw him slowly calm, my body started to tingle and warm beside him. My heart was an ache. I felt desire for him all the time. Like walking in and out of little storms every day.

As if reading my mind, he turned to look at me, one eyebrow quirking.

The narrow path of smoothed soil led through flickering ceilings of leaves, branches rising and giving birth to birds that took off like small, gray puffs of smoke toward the high, bright top of the massive building.

We talked of what we saw at first. "It's lovely here." "There are 500 species of birds here." "This ecosystem looks wild but it's really carefully controlled."

We kept our voices low in tone, hushed, and they felt almost like caresses even when we drifted back to the problem at hand.

"I want you to talk to me about what you're feeling, everything that you think you can tell me without discomfort."

He nodded.

"You trust me?"

Eyes so dark. "I do."

"This life of yours—you're going to get cold feet sometimes, you know."

"It's not—"

"I'm only saying that you must consider everything deeply. Not make rash, quick decisions, most especially if something is upsetting you. That makes sense, right?"

"Yes." He had his hands clasped behind his back, head bowed. Taller than me by a couple of inches, he made a very regal picture in his posture even if he might not feel like it in his mind.

"The palace is filled with visitors right now. I was attacked. There is a lot going on, a lot of stress and energy and force. A lot to deal with. And with the added change of the season, everything seems different. To me, at least. You should be used to it."

"I was not a part of that life for twenty years."

"Even in your pain-free hours?"

He shook his head no. "I did not involve myself. On purpose. I kept to the shadows. I was—my mind was—" it was hard for him to say the word. "—angry, frail."

"I understand that."

"Nothing mattered to me. None of it. You have to have seen it, all my feeling was behind a great barrier made by pain. Even when I didn't feel it, all I could think about was all that agony coming back night after night. The barriers could not come down. It was all I could do to hold together. The barriers held, and they held me back. Arku is the only one who could get through, and often he made no sense, insane as I."

He had not mentioned Arku since that fateful night when Nik and Arku dissipated into the Ghost Abyss.

I ached when hearing him speak of his dead twin.

I wanted to take his hand again. I didn't.

We continued to walk. It was easier to breathe while moving, especially when talking about difficult questions. We came around a patch of foliage, and through it we could see the rim of the building, the walls, constructed to look like natural rock, rough-hewn, shot with gold. Designed with careful precision to make them look like they were not designed with careful precision.

"My father," he said very softly. "I hated him."

"And now?"

"Resentment and gratefulness all mixed up."

"So for twenty years, no one dared to bother you. You didn't participate in anything?"

"No one forced me to do anything but endure the pain. The only force was in holding back the drugs to half-day doses for my own physical well-being, even when I begged for more. And strapping me down."

I pictured him aimless, a beautiful but cursed boy, at twelve, sixteen, twenty, twenty-five, haunting the palace corridors, reminding everyone of the fate of their realm, never moving forward. It had to have been a hideous thing to have your crown prince ghosting through palace rooms and halls, ineffectual, suffering, and remember your realm's fate every day upon seeing that because it was all embodied in him, a disaster of inconceivable proportions distilled into one royal, human figure who took it all inside him, a life of endless slicing pain, of screams, of death…or undeath. And less and less hope that any rift so grand could ever be mended.

It was no coincidence that upon my arrival, and my healing of the prince, everything was changing.

The hummingbird ship that brought me here was named *Harbinger*. That word describes one who is a precursor to major change. Or it could describe the foreshadowing of an event, an omen.

Me being here. It was no coincidence.

Funny how life worked that way. I could see foreshadowings in others when I was at the Temple. But never within me. Until now.

"So no one forced you to join the living even though you are a survivor." I thought about that, then added, "But you are clearly educated."

"Thanks to downloads, waves and computers."

His idleness had not been like that of a child, but of a caged being. He had had all he needed to sustain life, but no memory of a life. Ari was like new. Not blank, but fresh and open. In the midst of abrupt change, he was at his most vulnerable.

It should have been joy for him. I saw that in him only when we were alone. And at night, in our bed.

How I wanted to take him away, share in a plan with him to leave the Realm, make a new world that defined itself only through him and me, our entwining, our new love.

It was a traitorous thought.

"It's only been a matter of weeks, everything moving so fast. So you are feeling off. Today."

He frowned unhappily. "I haven't had time to 'be'. Everyone thinks I took a twenty year break and now I'm back."

"No. No they don't. They can't think that."

"I am not the person they think I am. I am not the person they want. Maybe not even the person you want."

I started to make an offended retort and stopped myself. I slowed my pace, forcing him to slow down. "Hmm. Maybe I haven't made myself clear enough?"

He looked sharply at me and when he did, I winked. That finally got a small smile from him and his cheeks flushed. "Yes. You have made yourself clear. " He put his hands up as if in surrender. "You always help me," he said, tilting his head. His voice came out thready and shy.

"Good."

"You clear my mind. You are clarity for me."

"Good."

He moved his head back, looking askance at me. "I think you were born with more gifts than healing."

Now that made me smile. It was a compliment I had not expected or been looking for.

"Everyone has gifts, Ari. More than one. Including you."

"But I have no time to even think about that."

I understood only too well why he had started this part of the conversation with the words: *I want to leave.*

What could I do about it? Be there for him. Give him clarity. It seemed like it wasn't enough.

"Maybe when things quiet down. When the delegations have left. Then there will be more time."

"Maybe." He glanced down at his necklace, picking it up from its chain around his neck, then looked at me. "My father wants me back."

I sighed. "You okay for now?"

He looked uncertain.

"Ari." I reached out and touched him on the shoulder. Lightly. My hand against the satin felt the warmth emanating from the skin beneath it.

"I need to go back." But his voice was toneless.

We turned to exit through the jungle the way we'd come, walking close enough that our shoulders brushed.

When I got back to our room, I went to my hand-screen and waved the king's coordinator, asking for an appointment with Kean for the following day.

9

The next day, mid-morning, Kean received me in an antechamber, not the throne room. I'd never been there before. As I'd requested, he saw me alone.

The floor was white, criss-crossed with black lines that, between them, created even squares of white. My soft boots made a slapping sound upon it. A huge crystal chandelier hung near an ornate, probably purely ornamental, hearth. The room's walls had murals of oceans, planets, moonscapes, very busy. Sculptures, large as a human, lined one wall, depicting nude men and women in varying poses. They looked old. The room was filled with stuff, relics and art, and smelled faintly of that oldness, musty but soapy-fresh as if it had just been cleaned by housekeeping.

Kean motioned me in. He was wearing all white, his sleeves long and fringed with white silks. His hair curved in a hundred silver braids.

He went to a huge wood desk, larger than any two ordinary desks combined, and sat in a tall but plush-looking chair. On the desk were gadgets, but also antiques such as candleholders, hour glasses, glass balls with fire in them.

A plush, plum-hued sofa faced the desk and Kean said, "Sit."

I was wearing my red coat and moved the tails aside as I sat.

Kean said, "I'm happy to have this chance to talk with you. You are a very special person here and I don't want you to forget that." Gray light from the window beside his seat etched him with an off-white aura, tarnishing his hair and white clothing. That light was strange and beautiful, and I could see dust motes floating in it.

"Thank you for seeing me. I know you're busy with everything, all the visitors. The holiday." My hands rested in my lap. I had the urge to twist them together. I resisted.

I had come to talk about Arulu, and part of me felt like a betrayer. The other part kept insisting I was only trying to help him. There was a gilt-framed mirror on a stand on a high shelf like a clear pool of water that reflected the ceiling and wall border. I focused on it trying to clear my thoughts.

I realized then that there was a silver-steel theme to everything in the room, including the king. Even the pure white of his clothing reflected odd pearlescent streams of light.

"Tahir, how are you feeling today?" the king began.

"I'm fine. I received treatment and the bruises nearly healed overnight."

"That's good to hear. I must apologize again for the attack on you. That is not tolerated here and I will see to it that it never happens again. We have all extra guards hunting for those men."

"Thank you."

"That aside, I hope things are going well for you," he said. "I have heard only good reports of the healings you have achieved."

"All minor. Your medical technology is beyond good. And people still don't quite trust me yet, despite what I did for Prince Arulu."

"So are you saying you want more work?"

"I'm fine for now. Still getting used to things."

"Of course." He put his hands on the desk. "And now, you had a matter to discuss with me?" Kean asked.

"I'm trying to think where to begin." I kept my chin high, my hands still. Inside, I hesitated. I felt suddenly wrong, embarrassed that I had come to the father to talk about the son who was my patient and my lover.

"Perhaps begin at the beginning," he said.

"I'm afraid this is a mistake." My heart fluttered. How could I talk to him about Arulu without perhaps insulting both men? I was completely out of my element.

"Is this about the prince?"

I swallowed. "I'm concerned for him."

Kean leaned forward, putting his hands on his desk. "You want me to be aware, perhaps, of the stress he is under. And I am. I appreciate that you are here out of concern for him."

"You do understand that current events make him—nervous."

"You are referring to my decision to take away the net, expose us to the larger galaxy again."

I nodded.

"The unrest from such change will be unavoidable, but temporary. But we cannot live shut away from other worlds any longer. We need outside trade to stimulate us. We need to sell our technologies, which are considerable, but remain un-liquidated assets as we stand right now."

So it was about money. Great decisions like this, based on economy, were beyond me. I knew little about governments and profit. Money had never been something on my mind. I understood how it worked, but I had had very little of it in my thirty years.

When I said nothing, Kean said, "Ari's nervousness will pass."

"You do realize that though he no longer feels pain, he has barely recovered. He has not had the time."

"He has you. Any problems with him I trust you will see to."

The muscles in my face felt tight. "Emotional problems can be helped with my gift, yes. But Prince Arulu strictly forbade me to touch his emotions in that way."

The king folded his hands and put them to his chin. "Then help him by being there for him. By supporting him. You do live together."

I felt my cheeks heat. "I do support him. I am here to ask if maybe he could have a break. Or if there's somewhere away from here he can go to relax. Just for a little while."

Kean looked thoughtful before answering, eyes glimmering. "You say you can help emotional problems with your gift? I need Ari here. He needs to work now. And he needs to be seen by the public. After twenty years—"

"I understand that." I had not meant to interrupt. The king looked a bit startled.

"I can order him to undergo treatment for his stress. Treatment from you. He is stubborn but in the end, disobedience from me would not be an option."

Now I knew for sure this meeting had been a mistake. If Ari was ordered by Kean to allow me to take on his stress, he would hate me for this, I was sure.

"There must be other ways," I argued. I had been in Ari's mind. I saw how tightly he held to his love for Arku, which was all tangled up now in his grief. To take that grief might dim the love. He would never allow that. I could not imagine taking that from him. "Besides, my alleviation of people's emotional problems with my gift is only a stepping stone. It gives them reprieve to find the energy to deal with their problem. It would be temporary." It was a half-truth. Often, emotional work by empaths was permanent.

"Then Arulu should have no problem. It's not as if you are taking something from him. I don't know why he would forbid you this action."

The king was obviously not hearing me. Ari did not want his emotions mucked with. That was his right, and only his, to decide.

"Your Highness, I truly feel that if he could just get away for awhile, he could get stronger."

"No. I need him. In this time of change more than ever." He sat forward, his hands dropping into his lap, the robes shushing against the chair. Patterns of icy light zigzagged the material at his chest. "I will make the order to him to allow you to heal his stress."

My heart hammered now. I began to actually panic. "I could try to talk to him first. An order seems like it's rushing a bit."

"You came to me," Kean pointed out. "I have seen his stress. It is noticeable. We are not rushing anything."

The way Kean spoke, as the king, with his dominance over everything, even this anteroom, felt like a physical force. It wrapped around me, giving me no out.

"I will make the order," he said firmly.

I inhaled, beginning to stand.

"And," he added, "the order will also be to you. Use your gift on him. No hesitation. I want him functional."

"No disrespect intended, but the problem will still remain. Unrest. People wanting weapons. And to hire mercenaries."

Kean's thick eyebrows rose, two silver moons down-turned on his face. "Of course they will remain. And as ruler of this Realm, I and my court handle those problems every day. In a professional and fair manner. With reason. Not caving to emotion. See that he functions in that capacity."

Then he smiled at me. I think I may have looked, for a moment, like I was caught in a sudden bright light.

"I know you'll do your job," he added.

I could say nothing to that. He was in command entirely. For him, the situation was handled, and he rose to hug me. His hugs were always warm and tight, heavy with his strength. But I now realized for the first time they were for greetings and dismissals. Not affection.

As he embraced me, he thanked me. Everything about our meeting looked good on the surface. But underneath I was shaking. For I knew, without a doubt, Ari would not cooperate.

*

I had made two promises. To Ari, I promised never to touch his emotions with my gift. To his father the king, I had

70

promised, as the official Palace Healer, to work under his command.

As I moved down the golden corridors my escorts fell into step behind me. Jackets of impeccable blue. Their hair woven and long. One dark, one light. I did not know these two, one male, one female, but they knew their job and didn't interfere with me in any way.

The Coming of the Light decorations gleamed silver, green, and red all along the walls. Garlands, ornaments and bells reflected the simmering light of the dragon sconces. Almost like being inside a dream.

I reached for my necklace to chime Ari. He didn't answer. I chimed him two more times with no result. I had no doubt he was busy. Or perhaps he had a reason to take the necklace off.

Despite everything Ari had told me yesterday about wanting to run away, he had had a good night last night. No nightmares. This morning he had showered and dressed as usual, making no reference to our conversation, no complaints. But I could still see a hesitation about him. A resignation, a flash of sadness in his eyes.

Of course, now I felt I'd been hasty at requesting a meeting with Kean. And that was not the least of it. I had not revealed Ari's secrets, but I had gone behind his back.

I had an appointment in half an hour to heal a fractured wrist. Medicine had already done much for the patient, but she admitted impatience with her injury and wanted a swifter release from her malady. It would be an easy process, minor enough that I probably would not feel tired afterward, but I'd still planned to go back to Ari's and my rooms for a quick nap.

I left him a message to meet me there, if he could.

Before my appointment, I cleared my mind by going to an open landing on the spiral staircase to watch the miniscule edge of a sun attempt to gain ground beyond the soft, ashen hills.

The sun was a silver curve on the horizon, and even with the darkened dome, still bright to look at. It seemed alive. It was contained within the net that surrounded all ten moons of the

71

September Stars and I could almost see behind it scintillation in the voids, a shiver there of the thing that kept us protected from the outside galactic reaches. There were never any stars to be seen through that shield. But soon there would be. I thought of it like a wall that went up and up forever. You could never see the top. And that wall was about to come down.

I breathed in. The air smelled of dryness, faintly chemical. Far to the north I could see part of the moonbase, its lights orange like hanging fires, its buildings gray and quiet, the landing field like a huge black tile dropped in the middle of lifeless rocks and sand. No ships were incoming. For the holiday, everything was quiet.

I tried to focus on my gift. I would be using it shortly. But thoughts of Ari would not leave me.

Finally, still distracted, I turned. My escorts followed me up to the palace guest level where I had stayed a short time upon arriving at Firgone. I instructed them that I would not need any special treatment for this minor healing, no immediate place to rest or quick food and drink. Back at the Temple, after an easy healing of this sort, I was always able to walk to my room on my own if I felt I needed a short recovery nap. Only the more difficult healings required assistance from others to a bed, and immediate sustenance.

I entered a lavishly furnished room to meet a small woman, her face covered in many wrinkles, her thin hair pulled into one small braid. She was dressed in fancy attire, a long brown leather skirt, so well worked and so thin it draped gracefully about her tiny frame. The blouse was lace with leather accents. She wore many rings and bracelets on one arm. Her other arm was wrapped with a white bandage and splint at the wrist. With bone knitting technology, she would heal in days. She didn't want to wait and I couldn't blame her.

She introduced herself as Kiera, and she said, unflinching, "My, you are a fine looking young man."

She assured me she knew about the kiss. "I consider myself lucky in two ways." She smiled. "You will heal me, of course. And I will have been kissed by a charmed young man."

"Good." I laughed. "I'm glad you think well of me." I sat before her at a small table. "Just so you know, my work is different for each patient."

"I'm sure it was a lot harder work to heal the prince," she agreed.

I nodded. I did not readily discuss patients with patients. "It won't hurt," I began, as I did with all my patients. "The process is painless. If you feel more comfortable lying down, that is all right."

"No," she said. "If we can sit here then that will be fine."

"I need to move closer to you."

"All right."

I slid my chair alongside hers. "I will touch you alongside your face with my hands to establish initial contact. Is that all right with you?"

"Of course, my dear."

"The gift is in mingling breath, and the kiss lasts as long as it needs to in order to make sure your injury is secured within me. Your body will find the path to being completely healed almost immediately."

"I am looking forward to it."

"Some of your thoughts may be vulnerable at this time. But I am trained not to read them unless it pertains specifically to the injury and the healing. For example, I might catch a glimpse of how you injured your wrist because I will be taking that part of you into myself. The gift does not erase memory. Also, everything between us is confidential."

My stomach twisted at my own rule. I had told Ari the same thing. I should never have had that damned meeting with the king.

"Thank you for telling me," Kiera said. "What a remarkable gift you have. Why, reading minds—that is not a talent to be squandered."

"I don't really read minds. I see images. I can communicate that way if I have to."

"Did you do that for the prince?"

"Ah, that is a story." I smiled gently. "But for another time."

Our tenets were strict. We did not reveal to others what we saw or spoke of with patients. For Ari, his secret about Arku was not one I would never willingly reveal. Not even to the king.

"Very well," she said.

"All right. Then we will begin."

Kiera's head tilted in the affirmative, and up. I put my hands on either side of her face. Her wrinkled mouth was dry and relaxed, her breath, cool.

She stiffened once when my lips met hers. This was not atypical of an empath's patients. The procedure was more intimate than many found comfortable at first. All of us with the gift took care to prepare hygienically as well, from breath to teeth to shaving if we were male. We took care of our appearances so as not to intimidate patients, or have them recoil. The gift itself created its carriers as pleasing to most eyes to better facilitate the process, and I had been told I was handsome many times, though I did not see it in myself.

The soothing traces of my gift began immediately to enfold and comfort, and all patients, even the most hardened and criminal, the most timid or afraid, responded to this. The gift swelled up, a real force. It worked mind to mind beyond identity and human cultural programs. The deep pool of it, which mere words could not adequately describe, never failed me.

In her mind, I saw immediately how Kiera had gotten up from her night's rest and fallen putting on a slipper. I could see her in a dim, gray light, trying to hang onto balance until the last minute, and felt the anger she had with herself for losing the game. She was old. 180, or thereabouts. Still, there were many years left for her in this long-lived, human culture. Her body was sound, but the bones were thin and there was no empath's cure for very old age. That was not one of our gifts. But I could heal her fracture and strengthen her bones, and I could definitely take away her pain so her more frail body would not be dependent upon medication for the days it would take her to naturally heal with a bone-knitting treatment.

Her thoughts were emotional about the accident, but intelligent and calm in every other way. I noticed this calmer trait among older folks, and I actually looked forward to old age because of that.

I did not read her thoughts beyond the peripheral ones, but I did sense some anxiety directed at myself, and a mild concern. That made me smile against her mouth as I sought the direct conduit to her abiding ache, and the fracture in her wrist.

The gift pinpointed the location and extracted the problem, giving energy to sealing the crack in her bone and comforting her mind as it did so. Some people describe the sensation as being enveloped in a warm bath as their particular problem gradually recedes. Others describe it as a gust of cool wind that blows right through them, leaving them pain-free and cured.

When it was done, her eyes seemed to sparkle as she appraised me. I undid the bandage on her wrist, taking off the splint. "Young man," she said, "you must take great care of yourself and that gift."

I knew she saw the slight bruising leftover under my eye that the oil I'd used had mostly healed. Everyone in the palace had to be aware by now of what had happened to me, of the attack.

I merely nodded, still slightly dizzy as the gift worked through me to take her ache and diffuse it.

She raised her eyebrows slightly. "They do not understand."

She took my hand in hers and held it for a long moment. Her dark eyes, framed by little eddies of wrinkles, held my gaze until I looked away.

She thanked me and offered me a jeweled bracelet from her hand as payment. I declined, telling her I was on the palace staff, well compensated for my time.

When I left, I headed straight for the rooms I shared with Ari. The healing was minimal, but my body still craved a nap.

I chimed Ari, but he still did not answer. I left him a message. *I need to see you now.* A heaviness formed in the pit of my stomach. I hoped to speak to him before the king gave him the order for me to treat his emotional turmoil. The sense that I had betrayed his confidence would not leave me.

10.

A pale pink light bled through my closed eyelids. A slight chill edged the air of the room because Ari and I liked to keep it cool. I was snuggled under a soft blanket, hugging a dyed, brushed silk pillow. The faded trails of a strange dream left a tinge of loss behind. My heart beat heavy.

I heard the sound of metal ringing against porcelain. Smelled hot honey and faint mint and opened my eyes to a vision. Ari stood before me all in red and black with only a "V" of his white shirt showing. His dark hair swept his left shoulder. He looked vibrant, young, and his eyes were gentle on me as he held out a steaming teacup.

"You made tea?" I sat up. The covers spilled from my shoulders. I had taken off my coat and shoes and shirt. I still wore the white trousers I'd donned that morning.

"Well, why not? You are always helping me. You helped me so much, when I was more than desperate yesterday."

A pang shot through my stomach. But I was also relieved. I knew then he had not yet talked to his father.

"Are you rested?"

I nodded, taking the offered cup. "It was only a minor healing."

"The bruising on your face looks almost gone."

"I don't even feel it."

He sat against the edge of the mattress, watching me, his eyes drifting affectionately over my naked chest, then back to my face. My face heated. He didn't have to say or do anything; my response to him came naturally.

I looked down at my cup. The tea was hot against my lips, the steam flushing my face more, and I blew on it, slowly folding my legs so I sat more easily in the bed. When I tasted the tea, it was a perfect blend, just the amount of everything I liked. To get the mix just right, as preoccupied and introverted as he had been, Ari also had been paying attention. To me. Again I couldn't help but regret my betrayal.

"Thank you for this." I nodded at the drink. "It's perfect."

"Well, after awhile, I caught on to how you fix it."

I set the tea aside and reached out, clasping one of his hands to mine. "I have to talk to you."

"I know. I got your message." His free hand touched the pendant that swung below his heart. The hand in mine gripped with a pleasant strength.

My own pendant sat where I'd left it on the bedside table before my nap.

Ari seemed so much calmer than he had been yesterday. I was afraid now that telling him about my meeting with Kean would make him not only nervous again, but furious with me. I wasn't sure how to read him. We had known each other only a short time. I had been in his mind when he was still not himself, not yet healed. He was still dealing with a major grief that made him fragile.

"So I only have a short break. What was it you wanted to see me about?"

"Your father has so many demands of you even on the holiday," I stated.

He sighed.

I took a breath. "I don't know how to say—" I stopped as sudden worry gripped me, making me wince. "I think you're going to be mad at me."

"What? Why?"

"Because—because I had a meeting with your father."

"What about?"

"About you." When I saw his face fall, I hurried on. "I knew it was a mistake the moment I walked into his anteroom. I'm sorry. I should never have discussed you with him without telling you first."

His brows narrowed, but he kept his hand tight in mine. "I suppose because my father hired you, you have to talk to him about me."

I shook my head. "No. What's between us is private. All of it. The healing. Everything. Most especially--" I softened my voice. "—Arku."

"Thank you for not telling him about him. But he's paying your salary. And I'm his son. He'll want to know everything."

When I did not respond quickly, he added softly, "Tahir, he would expect progress reports."

"Yes. He does." I pressed my lips tight, looked down. "But I want you to know that you can trust our confidences completely. But yesterday—" I took a deep breath. "You scared me. I thought I needed to do something."

His mouth formed the beginnings of a scowl. His voice came low. "I was overwhelmed by your attack and all the visitors. Too many strangers. The big celebration. I still feel it, that flight instinct."

"I know. I wanted to ask him if he could give you some time off."

"Nothing wrong with that," he said slowly, as if thinking it over.

"Well, that didn't go over well with him."

"It wouldn't. Kean is exact and demanding. He's a workaholic. He expects no less of me."

"But he asked something of me. And I can't – I won't obey him."

Ari frowned, the smooth eyebrows beautiful beneath his long hair that fell sideways across his forehead. A month ago this man had been a cold child trapped in endless loops of horror and pain. Now his dark eyes had depth. I would never tire of looking into them. He smiled and the faint, remaining shadows in them wavered. "I'm familiar with disobedience where my father is concerned."

"Yes, but you're his son. I'm in his employ. It's different."

"What did he ask of you?"

"He wants me to monitor and ease your stress. Ease your emotions with my gift."

For a moment, Ari looked as if he did not hear me. Then, all the beauty of him soured. His face closed in. He pulled his hand away from my grasp and looked directly at the window, saying, "You can't take them from me. My feelings for Arku—my grief—it mine! You promised me that."

"Ari, I know." He did not move or even flinch at my agreement. He kept staring at the graying light of the window.

"Both my mother and father know grief too well. Its sufferings. Its unrelenting pain. It changed them. Did they ask you to take away their pain?"

"No." I swung my legs over the edge of the bed. "I first made a promise to you, Ari. Not to touch that. Not to touch your emotions but to let you have them, even if they are painful."

He turned his gaze on me, shuttered now, swimming with deeper liquids that reflected the outside silvers of the slowly encroaching, half-year-long day. "You'll lie to him?"

"Not exactly. We'll work on your stresses in other ways. Together. I'll be helping you, just not the way he thinks."

"But I don't need to work on it." His gaze flashed. "I feel the way I feel. It's not wrong. They know that." His breaths came a little quicker. "But they don't know I hate being who I am. I never told you that. I never told anyone." He stood now, away from the bed, fists clenched. He faced the door, not me. "How can we work on that? It just is. Tahir, how can I fake to my parents that I don't want to eventually become king?"

I kept my tone gentle. "Well, what is your plan, then?"

"I don't have one. I never had to have one before you came. The chances of me recovering were zero. I never thought beyond my pain. But now, since you, everything's different. You took away problems, of course, but you left more in your wake."

He had said this before. Even about our love and the new, strange feelings that had awakened in him.

"I thought you'd work with me, not against me," he said.

"I'm not against you."

He stood tall and still, but I could feel his anger, and still so much mental pain.

I pushed my bare feet upon the cool floor to stand directly behind him, but I didn't touch him. "I'm not against you," I said again.

"I can't believe you told my father about our talk yesterday. Did you tell him I wanted to go away?"

"No. I didn't tell him anything. I only asked him if you could have a break, some time away. I made him think it was my idea." I swallowed thickly. "He refused."

"Of course he would. There's too much going on. The holiday. The decision to dismantle the net."

When he said that last, his right fist jerked. His back hunched, shoulders up, a defensive pose he held when I'd first met him, before I'd even begun his healing.

"I believe you have not had time to recuperate," I said.

Slowly, he turned but still would not meet my eyes. "I haven't. But my father doesn't care. He sees you as some cure all, and you can take care of everything perfectly. Even take away my feelings."

"Actually, it doesn't work that way." I so wanted to reach out and touch him, but I made no move toward him. "The gift, when dealing with emotional problems, softens the extreme, overwhelming parts. Makes it easier to adjust. It doesn't turn you into a robot."

"But I *am* overwhelmed! Isn't that normal?"

"Yes."

"Then I don't want my emotions softened. And what about my feelings for you? Would that soften? I don't want that. I'm afraid of that happening. I only just discovered those feelings, their intensity." Now he looked up and his eyes glistened. "It's wrong to even think of taking that." His mouth turned down and his eyes nearly overflowed. "The first time I was with you was like being hit by lightning. Different from the splinter-bomb. Something nice I never dreamed could be real. I want that to last. At least for as long as it can."

My stomach tightened to hear him talk about us as something possibly temporary. My brow tightened. "I would never touch that."

His eyes were so full now, but the tears did not spill. "And my grief. I hate it. But I need it. I'm afraid to forget Arku. I don't know what to do about that, but you're not going to take it."

"No. I already promised you." My heart was beating hard in my chest. My throat felt tense. I wanted to enfold him in my arms, go back to the way things were when he had stood so beautifully at the bedside, handing me a carefully prepared cup of tea.

I remembered the day I left the Onyx Temple to board the hummingbird ship. The sadness had been overwhelming, knowing I might never again see Zash or my brothers and sisters. It had been such a relief when Zash had kissed me and taken the edge off all of it. He had taken away the worst part of my grief of leaving. I was able to go forward, to function. I didn't suffer. I welcomed what Zash had done for me. I needed to be able to go on and do my work unimpaired.

I had healed many emotions in my time. Feeling had not been taken away from them. The patients did not become vacant, or tranquilized. But Ari didn't believe in this sort of healing, and I wasn't going to force it.

"I don't know what I'm going to do, but I'm not going to succumb to some easy fix," Ari said.

"I know that." Now I did reach out. I grasped his hand. He did not grasp back, but neither did he pull away. I said, "How do you think I dealt with the incredible change of leaving my home and coming here to live for the rest of my life? I had help. My mentor, Zash, he was like a father to me. He took the edge off my grief. He rarely did things like that with his gift. He never handled us that way growing up. He allowed all our emotions to be freely felt and learned from. But that day, before I left, he helped me with my overwhelming grief. It allowed me to come here. To do my job without distraction. For you. And I'm glad, because that led me to you. Him helping me with my job led me to something greater, better." I wanted to tell him I loved him, but I stopped short of that. He needed to hear my other thoughts first.

Slowly, Ari said, "I didn't know." Then his chin tilted up. "But that doesn't change my opinion."

"It's fine."

He was still frowning. "But didn't you feel deprived somehow? Of your feelings? Of the power behind them that has meaning only for you?"

"I was grateful, not deprived." But truthfully, I had never thought about it. Did the banishment of the worst core of my grief make me unwhole? Did it mean I loved my friends less? I didn't think so, but it was a good question, and Ari's thoughtfulness behind it surprised me. Perhaps I had not expected him to be so smart, so deep. But it wasn't as if he'd been in a coma for twenty years. He'd had time, even in great pain, to think very deeply, and probably about many things.

"All I felt for so long was only bitterness, anger and pain. Now I want to experience everything else beyond that. And my father is ordering you to take that from me."

"No. Not take it all away. Just help. But I won't use the gift to help you. I have promised you that. Ari—"

He interrupted. "I'm sorry I put you in this position. It isn't right after—after everything concerning me. The attack. All of it. I wish I could take you away. I would love for you to see Darkquill. I was there as a child and I still remember it like it was yesterday. The long winters. The snow."

I had not told him about the disapproval from three of the contingent from that moon. And I wasn't going to. Yet.

"The time will come" I said. *Just not now.*

Ari bowed his head. "I don't know how to do everything right. Or how you can help me make my feelings easier or even make them go away. I just feel what I feel. It has to be okay."

"Of course it's okay." I was horrified that he thought my gift might be part monstrous. But then I remembered it had revealed Arku, who had then achieved the freedom to leave his ghosthood behind. My gift had taken from him the person he most loved in all the known worlds. It would leave a negative impact. "I don't want you to feel awkward. Or as if you have to hide from me," I said.

Now I did move to embrace him. He let me, but his hands stayed at his sides. The silken texture of his clothing rubbed against my skin. I pressed my cheek to his hair, so cool, so smooth. He smelled of spiceberry soap. For all his past, long sickliness, he had strong shoulders and arms. He was wiry and fit. My arms around his shoulders tightened. I could feel the rise and fall of his chest, his barely contained uncertainty, a fragile innocence and the darker fringes of it that made him, like many people of trauma, wary, sad-edged.

"Ari," I whispered. "You can trust me. But if you don't quite yet, I'll do whatever I can to prove it to you." My eyes heated at my own words. My fingers twined into the hair at his nape.

Finally, his hands came up, his palms brushing the back of my waist, skin to skin, the barest of caresses. Where he touched, my skin seemed to sizzle.

"My father can be a very friendly and generous man, but don't be deceived into blindness at how demanding and manipulative he is." He whispered his words, as I had done.

He had mentioned the room might be bugged, but not the bedroom. I had a hard time believing it wasn't just paranoia on his part. But our privacy seemed even more necessary to me now. For him to completely trust me, I needed to be sure others would not interfere. With him. With us. But his status as crown prince meant we would never have any guarantee of that.

"I won't be deceived," I promised.

He moved his head back to look at me. His face came closer until our foreheads touched. "Good."

He tipped in to kiss me. I felt him smile as his lips parted against mine. That smiling kiss was everything to me. I had fallen for him hard. If he came to distrust me, I didn't know if I could bear it.

Something about him, more than anyone I'd ever met, pulled me in, like a planet to a sun. Even the echoes of his shadows and suffering compelled me. The depths of him. The many-layered darknesses. There was so much to him as yet unexplored. Somehow, the thought of it both chilled and thrilled me, along with his intrinsic blamelessness, like the virtues of a newborn. Combined with his shadows, his bitter ordeal, I was hooked. Maybe it was partly the healer in me, but more than that I knew he had a strength of will and beauty I'd only encountered in my deepest, most secret fantasies.

How I wanted him.

His fingers pushed against the waistband of my white pants.

When he pulled back, his breathing was deeper and his eyes were dark stars. "If I don't go back now, my father will chime me non-stop."

I smiled at him. "I know."

He raised his left hand between us and up to my face, pressing his palm to my jaw and his fingers to my cheek. He let out a quick puff of air. Gave a pained laugh. "Tahir, you make me want to—" He didn't finish.

I wished he would have finished. I craved to know everything he wanted.

I said, "I'll hold onto these thoughts until later."

He bowed his head, let out an exasperated groan, and headed for the door.

"Thank you for the tea."

He turned by the open door, and his smile was like the Coming of the Light.

11.

My own paranoia kept me in my rooms more than I might've desired. My bruises had healed. But there was one deep within me still, the fear of not being wanted here on Firgone, or any of the other moons of the Realm. It made me lonely, homesick.

The king ignored my obvious discomfort, or maybe he was oblivious. He always had me next to him and Ari at dinner as if to show solidarity toward me. But in truth, I had received few calls for my gift, and it wasn't because there were no brief illnesses or accidents, or that most of the big diseases had been wiped out genetically. It was because these people trusted their own medicine more than me, which had cured nearly every malady except what Arulu endured. I was an interloper. I had cured their prince, but beyond that they did not know me or need me. They did not want me in their rooms or their homes. I was like some anachronism to them. Someone from a different time. A sort of myth. They did not believe in me.

The Coming of the Light celebrations lasted ten days. But of course there were the days of preparation that led up to it. And the lingering celebratory fires of electronic hearths around every corner, and digital flame. Ari told me the celebrations for the Coming of the Dark weren't much different.

To me it seemed the holiday went on forever. The sun had not yet fully crested.

Ari remained on his best behavior. I noticed when he drifted off in thought at dinner. When sadness would plague him he looked momentarily lost, but no one else seemed to pay his emotions much mind. Kean had taken me aside twice during two different parties, to make sure I was doing my job. I always lied, telling him things were under control, that I had worked on Ari and he would be fine.

But in my arms at night, Ari would tell me, "Here with you like this is the only time I am truly happy." At those times, the silver dawn through our open window would stripe his chocolate hair and send the mica-flakes of color alight in his eyes. Every day before sleep, the weirdness of that light made a sort of sepia cocoon for us, as if we were the only two beings in the universe. I would feel myself overcome with touching him, never quite getting enough of the bright hair and gold-brown skin, the textures smooth, hard, moist, soft. Tangled in each other and the bed-clothes, we had a talent for kissing for long minutes without seeming to breathe. Minutes might turn to hours as we'd fall asleep with our foreheads pressed together.

Every evening after dinner, when we'd retire to our rooms, I would always listen to him tell me of his day. I listened to his frustrations, his exasperations, his boredoms. His longings. That was the part I liked best because he always wanted me. I was his longing. I comprised everything he'd wanted but could never have in his adult life. Not just lovemaking and a companion, but a person who represented places other than the Realm. A human from another world, another part of the vast Milky Way. I represented distance from his perceived cage, his destiny as crown prince, his memory of a horrid attack and the deaths of his twin brother and his sisters. I was his ticket to the stars. An escape, of sorts, although I wasn't going anywhere. I belonged to the king.

It was natural for Ari to want to start a new life with me. I know I wanted that with him. But there was really nowhere we could go. Not without permission from the king. We were trapped. My job. His destiny.

Ari's nightmares continued, but not every night. When they were very bad, my gift rose up instinctively to help. I had to consciously push it back as I put my arms around him and pressed my face into his hair to keep from kissing his lips and activating the healing.

He rarely woke during those times. I never told him I wanted to take those nightmares from him. That I longed to do it. I kept my instincts for that a secret.

On the eighth night of celebrating the Coming of the Light, we sat on the bed under the dusky dawn and Ari told me his father had set the date for the lowering of the protective net.

"It's only two weeks away," he informed me.

I leaned against the wall below the window watching the weird light glow in his eyes. He lay back on the pillows, hair spread across them, his legs bent over mine which were stretched straight. He wore nothing but the sheet at his waist. I wore a twist of a bracelet he'd given me the night before – a holiday gift—made of metal mined, so he claimed, from the core of a dead star. I wore only that, and no sheet. Ari had his hand on my wrist and was absently petting the bracelet.

"Kean made his decision quickly, then," I said.

"It will involve yet another ceremony and a lot of security because many people are uncomfortable." Ari sent me a look of reproach. "Security means mercenaries. Alien mercenaries. In space and on the moons. I'm not the only one nervous about it."

"I know that." If I was not trusted here, people would hate the mercenaries from other worlds even more.

"I haven't told my father that I don't want to go to the ceremony," said Ari.

I turned my hand up and into his. Our fingers twined. Of course Ari would have to go. The king would not stand for his son not to be there. In fact, I could see that politically it would be awkward, if not a complete mistake, if Ari did not show his face at the biggest event for these people in twenty years. For prince Arulu, the only survivor of a ground zero splinter-bomb attack on the palace and planet of Lyric Prime, being present for the unveiling was imperative. Revealing themselves again to the rest of the galaxy after so long was a very big deal. It was going to be done eventually. It was simply coming sooner than expected. His presence would make people feel more secure about being seen, about doing interstellar business and trade again.

I kept my tone quiet. "Do you think he will make a big drama?"

"Yes."

"You know I support you, right?" I hesitated, waiting for his nod. When I got it, I added, "But you can see his point of view, can't you?"

His eyelids lowered. His thick lashes cast shadows on his cheeks. "He saved me by finding you. But for his own agendas."

"He cares—"

Ari interrupted. "I don't care about his point of view because he doesn't try to see mine."

"He loves you. Of course he tries."

Ari complained about his father a lot. Now he turned his head away from me. I immediately backed off, staying quiet. I needed to convince Ari to do what was best for the king and his own destined life. That was my job as the king's healer. It was why he'd brought me to treat his son. But my heart wanted other things. To see Ari smile more. To have a span of time where we could both just relax without agendas, orders, demands.

I felt his hand in mine give a little tug. I did not let him pull it back. Instead, I moved forward, looking down at him. I placed my free hand on his shoulder and knelt by his side. "Come here," I said.

He could never resist me. So far.

Ari lifted his head and shoulders, put his hands under my arms and pulled me down to him.

"No matter what you decide, I'll be with you. If you end up at the ceremony, I'll be at your side."

"I'm not going," he murmured, lips almost touching mine.

"Okay," I whispered, brushing my mouth against his. Dry. Chaste.

It was a betrayal to the king to speak this way. Duty tore me, but my veins burned for Ari alone. My love for Ari brought no questions into my mind. I still felt I'd betrayed him when I'd gone to the king to talk about his stresses. I was still angry with myself for doing that. I would do everything in my power to make him happy. To protect him. In that regard, I was not torn. But I was already not a very popular person in the Realm. If I fell out of the king's affections for not continuing to treat his son with my gift, what would happen to me? There would be no place for me except as Ari's consort. And if the king and queen did not approve, but Ari kept me by his side anyway, I would become the most hated of outworlders not only on Firgone, but within all ten moons.

I wondered if Ari had given a moment's thought to my point of view. But I didn't want to talk about that right now.

"I really do appreciate you, you know," Ari said, pulling back from my kisses.

"I know."

"I don't want you to think badly of me."

Frowning. "I don't."

"That I'm weak."

"I don't."

He started to tremble.

"Ari, you survived something horrible. You're the strongest person I know."

His eyelids fluttered. "My survival was an accident of fate."

"And now? Look at you. You function quite well."

"Because of you."

"Not entirely. You are strong, Ari. Don't ever think otherwise. I certainly don't."

I leaned back to see his features more clearly. He gave me a wry smile. "You're just saying that to keep me in this bed." The expression on his face changed to hesitant humor.

"You want to leave this bed?" I challenged with a grin.

He moved forward to pull me back down to him, arms winding tightly around me.

*

I shut the heavy velvet curtains because the silvering light was getting to me. I had a headache. At lunch I'd lost count of the glasses of purple wine.

The drapes had been open for weeks because we both liked to watch the white and green flickerings of the dome overhead. Now, as the drapes dropped and shut, dust flew out like wisps of smoke. Slowly, the motes landed on the bedcover. I took it up in my hands and shook it out, carefully remaking our bed.

I thought about chiming Ari to come have some coffee with me, but it had only been an hour since lunch. I sometimes felt I chimed him far too often, as bored as I was.

I didn't like watching vid-shows while he was gone because we did that together at night before bed. So most days I read until I was out of my mind.

No one called for me. I had no appointments. This morning, I'd already gone for a long walk in hydroponics. I'd forced my escorts to take the flights of spiral stairs on foot, because I preferred that to the hover platforms.

I was restless. I wanted something more to do. But beyond that, what I really craved was to feel like I belonged here. It would take more time. I knew that.

I fell back on the neatened bed in the now dark room, my mind dizzy, my heart racing.

I did not remember falling asleep and woke barely in time for dinner.

I readied myself quickly, but still felt lethargic, dull. I dressed in black trousers with a white shirt, and a long black coat, the tails almost reaching the floor. With my pale hair shining in smooth strands just barely reaching the collar, and my irises so light in coloring they were almost white, I felt gothic enough to go walking in the city of Xia, which I wanted to visit again soon. I sometimes still thought it strange to wear clothes like these, but I also thought the fashions of this realm to be beautiful.

Lately, Ari had taken to wearing white shirts, too, with lacy red jackets lined with black satin. They accentuated his darker coloring, and I made sure he knew it pleased me.

I knew he liked me in scintillating purples and greens, but after my attack and the ruination of my favorite coat, he did not pressure me away from the blacks and silvers and whites I now preferred.

When I entered the giant banquet hall, my escorts stayed close. In fact, they would not venture further than a few feet away even as I ate my meals within the safety of the crowd and the king's table.

If possible, even more gilt and gaudy decorations were scattered about the vast hall as the festival was coming to a close. This was day nine. There were more garlands on the walls than ever, and new gold balls of all sizes on the tables. Sconce light filtered everywhere. Fake flames. Branches of green and brown hung from the ceiling up and down the length of the room, draped with glass crystals of every hue. Light danced behind ruby glass on side tables. Everything was flickering, even the people, a colorful mass of silks, leathers, tapestries, brocades.

Ari saw me from across the room. He looked slightly flushed, put out. He frowned at two people at his side, spoke rapidly, eyed me again and nodded for me to approach. As I came toward him I heard him saying, "…the mercenaries are the burden caused by hasty, greedy decisions."

One of the strangers said, "They come with their own set of dangers."

"Too late," Ari said. "It must be. And if you try to convince my father otherwise, you'll be--" He swallowed, not finishing his sentence. A puff of air pushed from his mouth and his glaring eyes clearly dismissed them.

Ari turned toward me, trying not to scowl. "Tahir," he said, rudely turning his back on the two strangers.

I could tell at a glance he was doing his best to not show his tension, and apparent to probably no one but me, his breathing held hints of a tremor.

"You okay?" I asked.

Down low, where nobody could really see, he reached for my hand. He did not usually show much affection to me in a crowd.

But now he held my fingers in a tight grip. The cuff of his red jacket brushed against my wrists. "I'm going to go crazy if I don't get out of here."

"But dinner hasn't even begun."

Through gritted teeth. "I don't care."

He started to pull me toward the royal exit and my escorts looked confused.

"Ari, hold up."

"I need to leave before I explode."

"What happened?" I tried to keep my voice soft, but the cacophony of the room made it hard to hear.

"I don't care about politics. This realm, our Realm is dead to me. Has been for two decades. No one sees this about me. Or cares." His dark eyebrows tried to meet above his eyes. "They want a prince but they don't care about me."

"Slow down. What are you saying? What happened?"

His hand gripped mine harder. His eyes locked with mine and my heart revved up just as a hand clamped my shoulder.

Startled, I turned, and Ari's grip released.

Kean stood before me, a hundred silver braids crowning him, a solicitous smile on his lips. His eyes, though, were like dark ice. "Ari," he said, "go to the table. Dinner is about to be served. We'll be there in one minute."

Ari shifted from foot to foot. This time I saw the scowl twist his lips as he turned to go. He didn't try to hide it.

Kean said, after Ari was out of ear-shot, "Your job was to even his tempers at the very least." His smile kept the sting from his accusation of me not doing the work I was brought here to do. "He's been difficult today. Arguing with everyone."

I took a deep breath, resigned to stay calm. "Isn't he allowed to have opinions? Those, I'm afraid, I can't take away with my gift."

"Of course not. And you should not. But he upsets the courtiers, the delegates, and my guests when he raises his voice. This may be the way in other cultures, but ours is more well-mannered."

"Ari seems fine when he's with me, sir."

The king's left eyebrow lifted. "Well, I can't entirely believe that."

"Then our definition of fine is, perhaps, not matching."

"It's our language. The nuances, even with the downloads for learning them, aren't always crystal clear. But I do think I made it crystal clear that you were to use your gift to manage Ari. He is emotionally unstable. If you have not noticed, then you are not the healer I thought you were."

I pressed my lips tight.

"You have been helping him as I instructed, have you not?"

This was the third time in less than a week the king had asked me this question.

For that moment, nothing was crystal clear. I didn't quite know what the king wanted in the end. A robot for a son? "You want him well mannered? He needs an instructor in the social graces, then."

The king's smile left his face. Everything about him hardened and I had no idea why. "I need to remind you, perhaps. You are on my payroll. You work for me."

"No. You don't need to remind me."

"Then use your gift. He's wound too tight. Take the edge off. You informed me you are perfectly capable of that. And relieving his unhappiness. Please deal with him. It's unacceptable."

"After everything he's gone through—"

"He's cured. You saw to that," Kean interrupted. "Now finish the cure. Take the pain of his feelings, and that will be all I require of you. If you want to go home after that, I won't keep you."

Shock at his words sent a coldness throughout my entire body. I had never considered that he might send me away. Not for one moment. Not after everything I'd done for his son. My mission here was to stay on indefinitely. To live in the Realm of the September Stars.

If I were forced to leave, I'd be seen as a failure in my long-term contract with Kean and his Realm. I would not only be a disappointment to Zash and my family at the Onyx Temple, but to an entire realm, not to mention Ari, who would never forgive me for he would be trapped here by duty and would not be able to follow me if I were forced to go.

I felt my face heat; my cheeks began to burn.

Kean seemed not to notice. His smile returned. "I see dinner is about to be served. You will accompany me to our table?"

I blinked back the heat in my eyes, nodding. I followed the king to where Ari and his mother already sat, waiting.

Ari was looking down at his empty plate. His mother, preoccupied with her own thoughts, had a glass of sweet juice raised to her lips. She put it down and formally greeted the king, both hands up as he clasped them. I had never really had many words with her. Curious, still churning inside, I considered that I might need to remedy that oversight.

I sat beside Ari and said nothing. After a moment, he turned to me and said with a soft snarl, "My father does not like it when I don't share his exact opinions."

"I see that," I replied.

Kean turned from his wife and seated himself next to us, Ari on the inside, me on the outside.

The food was served. It was steaming and fresh, but I savored almost none of it. My vision wandered over the crowd at their lower tables, people chatting away, eating, drinking, There was both excitement and tension. A big change was coming after twenty years of silent recovery. There were bound to be shock-waves. Politically, personally. An entire culture in an upheaval of change.

Certainly I worked for the king. That truth could not be denied. But Ari was my patient, and my lover. My first duty was to him. It seemed I vowed newly, every day, that I would protect him no matter what. It was a promise my mind kept repeating every time I saw Kean, Ari, the visitors. Every time I read more articles about this culture. Its magnificent artisans and inventors. Its starship engineers. Its incredible scientific prowess. The history of internal violence and war now over a thousand years at rest. These were a civilized people, educated and smart. But even as I thought all of this, I felt my escorts at my back, close, alert.

Perhaps these people were right not to trust me. I was certainly an interloper. I had their prince in my bed. And because of my coming, everything was changing now.

It was changing for me as well, because their king had just now threatened to take all of what I had just gained away from me. Including Ari.

When I had first boarded the hummingbird ship to come to the Realm, I never expected any of this. I thought I'd live a quiet, solitary life, much like at the Temple, participating in healings as needed.

But now I had Ari, and something huge and protective within me woke.

I sat for a moment, still ignoring my food, then turned to Ari and, not caring who saw, leaned close to his ear and whispered, "Can we leave this dinner. Now. Please."

He turned his head, meeting my eyes, his face so close to mine I could feel his breath. "Yes."

"What should we say?"

"Who cares? Say nothing, if you like. We'll be noticed no matter what. Let's just get up and walk out and dare anyone to say a thing."

Defiance created conflict. Conflict needed to be avoided. "No," I said softly. "Follow my lead. Tell your father I'm sick." Then I leaned toward Ari, my head falling toward his shoulder, and nearly fell out of my chair against him. He caught me and stood abruptly, holding me up by the arm with one hand.

"Father, Tahir is not feeling well. I'm taking him back to our rooms."

Then, without waiting for a response, he lifted his shoulder under my arm and steered me toward the royal exit. Our escorts followed closely but remained silent.

I didn't care what they saw. Our escorts. They had seen enough already. When we were away from the crowd, I put my arm around Ari's waist and gave a short laugh.

"I'll have the kitchens bring some food down later, if you like," he said.

"No." I didn't whisper. I didn't care who heard. "I just want you." Then I turned in his arms and gripped his shoulders, kissing him on the mouth.

He grinned under my lips.

I pulled back. "I want you to trust me. I'm going to do everything I can for you, and not for your father."

His grin slid away and his eyes glistened. "Thank you, Tahir."

I pulled him forward to the hall and the stairs, knowing he'd want to avoid the hover and walk. "Let's go." I paid no mind to our escorts, and neither did he. I kept hold of one of his hands and we jogged down the spiral stairs.

"Rumors will fly now," Ari said softly.

"Let them."

"What about my father?"

"We're going to be careful with him, okay? We're going to have to plan carefully. Make him think I'm using the gift to keep your harsher emotions more complacent."

His face fell as we walked. "I've disappointed you in my lack of control."

"No. If you are to rule one day, you have to have your own ideas, thoughts and opinions. They can't all be just a reflection of your father."

"Thank you for saying that."

"It's just that he holds the power. And he doesn't believe me that even if I did obey him and gave you the kiss to make you happier, it wouldn't affect your opinions. Or your moods. He thinks I have some skill at controlling your entire personality, which I don't. Ari, we're going to have to play him right. Make him think he's getting what he wants."

"I've never done that before." He gave me a grudging smile. "I have always openly defied him."

"As many sons do. You're not different in that aspect."

"He thinks my condition made me difficult. Maybe it's as you say—just my personality."

I gripped his hand tighter. "Maybe," I said. "I don't have a problem with that. Yes-men are boring. But Kean has threatened me."

"What?"

I nodded to assure him he hadn't heard wrong. "He threatened to send me away."

Now Ari stopped abruptly, his hand pulling me into a skid on the hard floor of the landing between steps. "What?"

I had almost lost my balance, but he pulled hard to help me stay upright.

The four escorts, two for him, two for me, waited above, and about eight steps back, their midnight blue jackets shushing against their legs with the sudden stop. The light over the land beyond the stair wall glittered. The soft curves of the moonscape gleamed off-white, the distant hills shaped like the dark, frozen swells of a sea. Some of the hills sported ragged edges, like skirt or trouser hems come undone. Overhead, the dome was darkened to keep the intensity of the rising sun dimmed. It sparked as if scattered with pink and green glitter.

Ari's eyes were round with shock. "He said he would send you away?" His voice came out coarse, tight.

My skin chilled as I heard the words come from his mouth. As if saying them made them all too real. The air under the dome remained always a fairly moderate temperature, fluctuating little. Dry, warm, still. But now my skin was cool.

I let go of his fingers and walked to the wall, putting my hands on the hard stone that rose just above waist-level. The edge of the sun's disk was like a mirror. I almost thought I could see the reflection of the palace in it, dark and looming, two towers rising high, one for all the palace activities, one for all the private rooms and housing. In between, the giant throne room took up several stories on its own.

I squinted.

Ari said, "Tahir. He can't do that!" He came to stand beside me.

"I think he can."

"He knows that would make me defy him even more."

I turned away from the sun. "And then what would he do?" I watched the muscles under his eyes shift, his cheeks twitch.

"What he's always done with his sick son."

I frowned.

"Medicate me. Stuff me away somewhere and take me out whenever he needed to show me off."

"No. Kean isn't like that."

"Tahir, the splinter-bomb didn't just injure me. It injured us all. It killed my brother. My sisters. It made my parents lose their light. And so many people on all the moons as well. But my parents rule. My father takes care of the politics. My mother is the business end of things. Either one of them, apart or together, is capable of whatever it might take to see their realm evolve and grow. To say 'Kean isn't like that' is to say you don't understand his position, let alone who he is."

98

"Okay. I've only seen him as friendly to me, until today. And I see him as your loving father. I admit that."

"I have often questioned the love part."

"He does, Ari. I know he does."

Ari shrugged. "What I'm saying is that he threatened you because he sees you as a threat. There is no other reason."

"And for control," I added. "He wants control over you most of all."

"But I don't seem to be handling that very well, right?"

"We can do this together, though. You're not alone."

He pushed his lips together and looked down. "Thank you." Voice soft like a caress, as if overwhelmed.

The way Ari's emotions played so rapidly all over the board fascinated me. As if the truth inside him, all about who he was, what he felt, thought and stood for, had been released. Before that all he'd ever known since age ten was pain, or the promise of pain to come after his drugs wore off.

I had read up on his case, all that I could find. There were sketchy details, but they were horrible. He was found clutching the pieces that were left of his dead twin, Arku, and covered in blood. His own flesh had been torn to ribbons up and down his torso, nearly all of his bones broken. His face had been spared because he had hidden it against the chest of his twin. At least that was the conjecture. Technology put him physically to rights, and after I discovered how extensive his injuries had been, I marveled in bed at how flawless his body was, completely scar-free. As if he'd never been touched by pain, injury or illness a day in his life. The skin and bone-knitters would have taken time, but they put him back together seamlessly, growing new tissue inside and out.

Now that Ari was himself again, it was important that he give voice to and express his emotions. My gift could help him ease into them, of course. Taking the edge off his nightmares was one thing I longed to help him with. But he did not want that and I respected his wishes.

"Ari," I said. "We'll work out scenarios to make your father think I'm using the gift on you. I want to be at your side more. We can work out systems on how to deal with when you are overwhelmed. Exercises. Signals from me that I am supporting you. We need to work together." I lowered my voice. "I can't bear to be sent away."

"No. I won't allow that." He reached for my hand again.

The light reflected pale blue in his hair, always loose, down. His red coat was fitted at the waist, showing off his lean angles. I wanted to pull him to me.

I took a deep breath of the dry air. Somewhere in the distance came the high-pitched howl of a ship landing at the now open moon base. It was the loneliest sound. I moved away from the wall. Ari followed, dropping my hand.

I said to him, "Do you really think our rooms are bugged?"

"I don't know."

"Maybe there are ways to find out."

We headed quickly down the stairs, round and round.

"I want the curtains to stay closed tonight," I said.

"What? Okay," he replied, looking at me with questions in his eyes.

I would do my best for him with everything. To remain in his life, I had no other choice. But because he was all I wanted now, I would have done it anyway, for no other reason than love.

12.

It was amazing to lie in the darkness, get away from the light for a while. The room's shadows curved about us, friendly and warm. Ari slumped against my shoulder, his body pressed tightly to my side. His breath heated the skin of my neck in an even ebb and flow, informing me he was asleep. I felt

100

completely relaxed and should have been on the verge of sleep myself, but I was wide awake.

We had talked long into the night. Of politics I still struggled to understand, and which Ari could not have cared less about. Of Kean's obsessive need to control all about him, despite the friendly and disarming mask he showed to the public. Of Darkquill, Ari's favorite moon where he told me should he finally become king decades down the line, he wanted to build a palace.

I still had not told him of the three in Darkquill's contingent who had disapproved of me.

My arm was under Ari's neck and curved up over his back. My fingers were woven in his hair. My other arm crossed my own stomach and rested on Ari's naked hip. I had pulled the sheet up to our elbows.

I couldn't see him in the darkness, but I could feel him, heavy and trusting beside me. When you made love without light, or in the faintest stirring strobes of candles, skin felt softer, kisses more feathery, heady, drugged. There was a huge difference between sex and making love. Much as I'd liked and enjoyed Nik, I had never known that until meeting Ari. Nik and I had had sex. Ari and I had something else. Something that made my throat ache and my heart thrum.

I turned my head and pressed my lips to his forehead. Just a touch. A way to feel that thin skin over the skull, and the glossy filaments of errant bangs. It was the closest I would come to the entrance of his mind now. In this state, I dared not touch his lips. The gift might rear. I'd only recently found out it responded to love in unpredictable ways, such as worry, anxiety, and concern. I kept those feelings away when making love with him, and so far I'd managed to kiss him with impunity.

My promise to him was sacrosanct. No gift. Not without his permission. Not unless absolutely necessary to heal a malady or injury.

He did not want me in his mind. Who could blame him?

I would not betray him again.

*

The next morning we ate and bathed and dressed together, and left our rooms together.

The extra decorative light of the long hallways cast Ari into a glimmering mirage of golds and reds. I had chosen to wear all black underneath a violet coat. Aside from my wintry hair, I absorbed the shadow more than the light.

"I am not invited," I insisted to Ari. The meetings were for delegates and the royal court. It was the third time I'd made this statement to him.

"You are technically part of the court; you have a title. And you are invited. By me." Amazingly, Ari swept through the halls like the prince he was, wrapped in a sort of automatic self-assurance that came with living here for so long, but also, I could see, from being born to it. Despite not wanting the power, he had all the trappings of a king. They simply weren't stitched together yet. He had so much time to come into his own. To grow. To make his own decisions and learn who he was. Kean was still young by the standard life-span of these people. Though he had had his children in his sixties, ninety was considered middle-aged. So why the king seemed in a rush to control Ari was a puzzle.

"I am not trusted. I'll be in the way." I was having second thoughts about attending the meetings, talks, council gatherings and throne room rituals.

"It doesn't matter. You are trusted by me and entrusted by my father to me. If I say you are needed to ground my well-being, he can't argue. He did, after all, command it from you."

"Just because I am there doesn't mean your behavior will be controlled," I said, letting out a laugh to soften the criticism.

He didn't seem offended. "It'll remind me that we have a higher calling." His smile, thrown back at me under the garish lights, was brighter than anything around us.

We still had no discernable plan other than getting Kean off Ari's back, and off my back (along with the threat to expel me), as well as making Ari feel more confident under his father's imposing kingship. After only one night's worth of scheming, it had to be enough. For now.

We came into the throne room which was decorated in golds and blues within an inch of its life. It was the first meeting of the day for Ari, and we ran into throngs of delegations from the nine sister moons. There was to be some kind of special law signed, and monies to be dispersed for protection to each moon based on their population, and their worth. I knew nothing of the technicalities of it, only that they had no armies of their own, and were hiring outside protection for business commerce, and to protect the rich mines that were the focus of three of the larger moons.

I knew that when you had something valuable to trade like artistic starship design, and star-drives that made space travel look like magic, you needed protection from crime. They had had free trade without incident for centuries before the alien splinter-bomb attack and destruction of their system. But they were not going to make any mistakes this time around regarding safety.

The issue was trust.

The galaxy was no longer seen as worthy of that, or completely benevolent.

Yet, there had been no big wars in the entire galaxy in its recent history spanning a thousand years. The splinter-bomb attacks of unknown origin had happened seemingly randomly, and only three times in different sectors in three hundred years. I had read up on that. No one knew why they had happened. No one had ever been able to ascertain the source, or name the alien instigators. They always pillaged the planets they attacked, and destroyed them afterward.

Ari had informed me the delegations were split, even within their own ranks, some wanting mercenaries and outside armies to patrol their realm's space, some wanting nothing to do with soldiers, or warships, or star-weapons constructed with only one reason in mind: to destroy.

The galaxy had been at peace for longer than most could remember. But skirmishes still existed, and civil wars localized to single planets. And there were legacies of pirates in almost every sector. But the decision stood. The Realm's ports would be open to outworlders. Strangers would be free to come and go for business and personal purposes. Mercenary companies existed to supply protection in these areas where a person, a nation, or a conglomerate of moons might feel the threat of danger.

His Highness, Kean, King of the Realm of the September Stars, had hired an entire battalion.

But with extra money allotted, each moon could also afford to employ their own personal mercenaries and guards as desired. So in addition to the battalion, they could have their own security, personal and trusted on a separate payroll.

The decision about the net had already been made days ago. Whether people liked it or not, it was coming down.

Ari supported the battalion. It was one area where he and his father agreed. They had a ready fleet of hawkships that could easily be redesigned to accommodate the soldiers. The hired battalion came with its own ships, but Lyric Prime starship technology was far superior. Very few citizens of the Realm had voted against using the hawkships; they wanted that superior science in action. And using their own ships was a matter of pride as well.

The signing of the documents for the battalions and protection money involved much ritual and time-consuming aggrandizing. Special quilled pens were used. The documents themselves were like marble, flat, thin and shining. I wondered if they were paper-thin digital screens. They did not fold but came in ornate, quilted envelopes.

The regents each had their turn, bowing, signing, making short "thank you" speeches. It took forever.

104

Ari stood, hands clasped behind his back, beside his seated father. Mostly he looked straight ahead. Sometimes I saw him glance down at the table at the documents at his father's hand and the quill he held.

I found a bench off to the side and stayed behind the throngs.

My escorts followed dutifully. One of them today was Sullen, one of the first guards I'd met upon my arrival months ago, and who had helped me during my assault. Most escorts never spoke to me. Sullen always nodded to me, and said, "Hello." Sometimes he even found moments to insert comments into my day. I hadn't seen him in awhile, and it was a welcome relief to find him at my side again.

It took nearly an hour for the ceremonial signings to be completed. During that time, Sullen inched toward me and started a soft dialog, beginning with asking how I was, and apologizing for being away since I'd been attacked.

I wanted to lie to him. Instead, I admitted a truth. "I've healed all right, but I confess I'm feeling a bit unwelcome here lately."

"But you have Prince Arulu's trust. The entire Realm supports him."

"And the king's trust," I added, trying not to make it sound like a question.

"Yes. Of course."

"Sullen." I lowered my voice. "What have you heard?"

"Some believe the king wastes his money and time on you. Rumors abound he might send you away. Of course he reveres you for what you have done for his son. You wouldn't be here in this room right now if it were otherwise."

"I am not here at the king's behest."

"The prince's, then?" he asked.

"Yes."

"I have no orders to keep you away from the king's dealings. But usually it is his and only his request that summons or dismisses people from his court."

"In other words," I said, "they don't come and go as they please."

"No."

"Would you remove me, then?

His kind face took on a horrified look. "Not at all. I'm here for you."

"Until the king commands otherwise," I added.

"Until the king commands," he echoed.

Sullen remained at attention to my left. The other guard who looked barely out of boyhood, said nothing.

After just over two hours, the crowd began to disperse.

I saw a flash of red, dark hair like flame as it seemed to absorb all the lights. Ari headed in my direction. I could not see the king from where I sat.

Ari approached and said, "He gave me a look."

"A look? You mean Kean?"

He nodded. "I'm sure he'll be over here in a moment."

I stood, straightening my coat which suddenly seemed too thick. It was hot in here, I realized.

It took awhile for the king to make his way through the crowd as he shook the hands of delegates and regents alike, and smiled in every direction. When he finally came to us, he was looking directly at me.

I tried to remember how tightly he'd hugged me, the moment he'd given me my title and how much that made me feel I belonged. How he treated me like a foster son even now, and had me at his table every night with Ari and his wife. One of the family.

But in his eyes now, I could sense a change. He kept his smile but his brows narrowed as he said, politely, "I do not remember your invitation."

Ari stepped forward. "I invited him."

Kean looked away to his son. "Indeed."

"I'm informed you wanted him to monitor me as to my, uh, behavior," Ari said. "While I'm still at a loss as to why my agitation at your decision to remove the net is wrong-thinking, I nonetheless brought Tahir along to make sure I don't throw myself at your feet and embarrass you with a tantrum."

I was aware of every sound, now, every clink of heel on the marble floor, the lilt and tone of every voice in the room. There was receding noise as people exited, and echoes of lively discussion from those who had not yet made their way out. Yet, it seemed I could also hear the flicker of each tiny spark of fire in every dragon sconce that lined the walls.

I saw all the muscles of Kean's face go rigid under his lightly wrinkled skin. His coat, all of white dotted with patterns of crystal-white stars that twinkled in the room's myriad lights, shifted slightly against the smooth floor.

"Good," he said calmly, though he was anything but calm. "Then hopefully your rationality has returned at last so that I won't feel I'm being continually shadowed by a child."

Ari's fingers curled. He said nothing.

Kean turned his gaze once again on me. "Tahir is welcome, of course."

"Thank you, your highness."

"Kean. You are to call me Kean. I've told you this."

"Yes, Kean." I made myself smile, trying to forget that only last night he'd threatened to have me sent away.

"I expect you to respond to any problem that might evolve."

"My gift does not take away all emotion," I tried to explain.

"No, of course. But unfounded fear and anxiety are treated by your kind, the empaths, yes?"

"Yes."

"Excellent. There should be no further problems then."

I stole a quick glance at Ari who had the audacity to roll his eyes. Luckily, his father did not see. All around me were glowing branches, streamers strung around columns and draped in curves along the carven walls. The two thrones themselves glimmered with gilt arm-covers and gold, over-stuffed back cushions.

As usual, Winter was not in attendance. Ari informed me she rarely came to any of the meetings or political ceremonies, busy with her computer programs, and over-seeing the Realm's glorious wealth from the past, making sure it did not dwindle too quickly. We saw her only at some meals.

As the king turned, leaving with his entourage, Ari leaned in and said to me, "My fate is sealed. My destiny is to die of boredom. And annoyance with my father. Is there a cure?"

"Not sure." I let out a sigh.

"There will be several more meetings like these before lunch, but smaller scale in the king's anteroom. The paperwork for the hawkships is no small task. He has assistants see to it, but they require signatures. And witnesses, including me. "

"Onward, then." I followed him out. Our escorts stayed directly behind us.

We made a day of it. I didn't feel too useless for a change. Being with Ari made everything better. At least I felt wanted by someone in the Realm.

Lunch could not come quickly enough.

It was the small banquet room that was used today. The light from the high windows reminded me of the Temple and home in winter, the way the gray skies would cast the land and the rooms in lonely, tarnished splendor. The rooms at the Temple had been not nearly as spectacular as the palace, but they were high-beamed, some of them big and empty enough to be filled with echoes and the scent of ages.

A knot formed in my throat. I didn't want to go home. Yet I was torn. I missed it, and a longing for it swept me up. At least I had belonged there.

Ari was about ten feet from me, talking quietly to a delegate, on his best behavior and possibly not faked because my presence really did make him stronger. Sullen stood closest to me, and my other young escort stood six feet behind him.

Sullen said, rather out of context, "I think you are doing very well."

"What?"

"I just think," he answered quietly, "it must be very very hard. And it's a holiday. You must've had family somewhere, at some time. The people you are used to being around whom you love."

I turned to look at him. His eyes were dark agate green. They peered into me with a kind of invisible light that I could feel, a shaky tourmaline zig-zag like a hesitant arrow, slow and fumbling.

"You read emotions," I said.

"Of course. It's quite easy."

I realized I was looking at a man with a gift, completely untrained. We had two of them at the Temple. They were excellent hosts for the healing business. They read moods and automatically put people at ease.

Sullen was like them, but he did not think twice about it. It made him instantly intense, but likeable. Now I understood why I had felt affection for him immediately when we'd first met.

"Ari is doing well today," he commented casually.

"You can see that?"

"Yes. Can't you?"

I could, but I could not always be sure of his inner turmoil unless we were alone together and he was talking, letting down his guard. I wasn't great at seeing lies. Ari had promised me he would behave. That promise did not mean he was authentically comfortable and relaxed within himself.

"Today the grief is not such a bundled shadow about him," Sullen observed.

I don't think Sullen realized how special his words were to me. Or maybe he did. All I could think as I looked at him was that his guard duties were wasted on him. He should have been an ambassador, or something equally grand and important.

The edges of his lips lifted. "You are doing well, just know that," he said again.

"Thank you, Sullen. Thank you very much."

He nodded at a point behind my shoulder. "The king wants you to go to the table now, I think."

I turned. Kean was motioning for all his guests to sit. The room quieted a bit as everyone found their places.

I sat on the king's left this time, Ari to his right. Winter had not made an appearance. I missed sitting next to Ari, but often that happened at the lunches I attended.

Behind me, I felt Sullen's strong presence, and I realized I felt more at ease because of our conversation.

I was actually starving. I ate larger portions than normal.

Ari had an appetite, too. Kean noticed, looked pleased for a moment, and ordered the servants to serve us more.

At one point, Kean turned to me. "I know I said this morning you were not invited to the meetings, but now I would like you to know your presence is welcome. It has certainly had an affect on Arulu. Keep it up and there will be no worries for you."

"He has his own mind." I could not help but make the statement, trying to make him see his son was a man, not some thing to be compelled, not a subject that simply obeyed orders. But he was king. He lived and breathed orders.

I added, "But I'm doing my best." I would take the credit for both Ari and myself, though I had not touched Ari's mind since the initial healing of his relentless pain.

"Good. And you two are still happy together?"

I had been swallowing as he asked, and the food almost stuck. The last thing I wanted was to ever talk about our personal life with Ari's father. "Fine," I said, voice a bit scratchy.

"I have not thought about making any announcements. Ari was always the shy one even as a child. But it is not unusual for the men of my line to prefer male life partners, and it's completely culturally accepted. I myself—"

"Father," Ari interrupted from the other side. "Stop it."

Kean looked miffed at first. He turned toward Ari and said, "Stop what?"

"It's only been a couple of months and you're trying to engage him to me?"

"It's all right," I said under my breath.

"Well, you live together," Kean emphasized.

"I don't care." The words came hot. Ari banged his knife against his plate a little too hard. "Stay out of it."

I felt my chest constrict at his words. We had never discussed commitment, not even when we had moved in together. But the thought of Ari being insecure about our future pained me.

I remembered when I'd first arrived on Firgone that a medicated Ari had argued roughly with his father in front of me. Before I had discovered the extent of Ari's condition, I had wondered then if I had been called to mediate a father-son dispute.

I wasn't so sure now that I hadn't been correct in my initial assumption.

Their personality conflict back then seemed to have stemmed from Ari being resentful that his father had gone to great lengths to save his life. For Ari it prolonged his suffering. But now that Ari did not suffer, it was obvious the father's general control over the son was the issue.

Of course I saw it clearly in my meeting with Kean. It was why I'd felt so badly afterward. Why I'd feared I'd betrayed Ari's confidence.

"Your life is of interest to me," Kean said to Ari, voice casual, as if he were doing nothing but showing his love and concern.

"My personal life is my own," Ari said, staring hard at his plate.

"Of course, but as your father, can I not show an interest?"

Ari fumed silently, not answering.

Kean turned to me. "I show an interest and it is wrong?"

I looked at him straight on, thinking hurriedly, *Do not allow this attempt to be placed in the middle.* "Maybe you should ask him if he wants it public yet. Or to even discuss it. That's all he's saying."

Ari lifted his head, sending me a grateful look.

"Of course I would ask him first." Kean looked at me as if my logic was suspect.

I refused to let my blood heat up. "Of course," I echoed.

"And," Kean continued, his dominance apparent in his inability to let the subject go. "I was only trying to communicate that all of it is fine. Expected. The men in my line tend to prefer men. Winter and I expected this for Ari. I have had consorts of both genders, but I eventually preferred to marry Winter. That was forty-five years ago."

"Forty-five years." I was impressed. I focused on that, and kept my mouth shut about the argument that most studies showed children were bisexual in nature if they weren't culturally programmed to be otherwise. The king's bloodline was not a factor.

"Ah but if she weren't queen, I suspect she'd have cut our tie some time ago."

"Father!" Ari said.

"Ari is uncomfortable discussing personal matters in public. He was like that as a child, as well. But this is not news to him."

Ari looked up and said, through gritted teeth, "No, it's not. I know you and mother do not spend much time together. But this is a public lunch. And if she were here, you wouldn't have said it."

"I might have," the king argued gently.

Ari let out a short breath of disagreement.

"Can I discuss anything you ever approve of?" the king asked tightly.

Ari replied, "Maybe not."

I winced. I so wanted to go to him, put my hands on his shoulders and just whisper to him, *Relax, I love you.* For his own sake, not mine, I wanted to soothe him, though perhaps the king would blame me for Ari's sass and not just his anxiety and misunderstood grief.

Kean turned to me again. "If you ever have sons, I wish for you ever-enduring patience."

Ari made a face, as if he'd just eaten dirt.

I wondered if this was how it had gone every day that I had wandered the halls alone and not been there. Every day that Ari had been directed to attend meetings, and council sessions, and kingly rituals, and then come to our rooms at night frustrated, angry, wanting to run away.

I had not been raised by parents or blood-relatives, but I knew this kind of discord existed in every family, no matter their make up. I was grateful for my wonderful relationship with Zash, but I'd had my rebellious moments. They had been small, as I was not too strong-tempered, but those moments existed. The Temple had been a different environment, though. I had my foster brothers and sisters to take the edge of any prolonged focus. I looked up to Zash, loved him, but he did not have the time Kean did to devote all his energy onto me.

And then there were the special circumstances between Kean and Ari. Not normal. Not ever normal. How could they be? Five of Kean's children had been murdered by a horrible invasion. Ari had survived only to suffer for two long decades. Nothing here was normal. Even with the help of time, it never would be.

I took a deep breath and turned my focus toward eating my steak. Cooked to perfection, it melted in my mouth, the one thing that had gone right this day.

13.

Ari watched me rise from the bath. He lay back in the still-hot water, not yet wanting to leave its comfort. We'd been discussing the day.

"Ugh. My father's job. I am going to die of boredom," he breathed, fingers weaving through what was left of the suds and bubbles. The ends of his hair floated on the surface of the water all around his chest. His eyes followed my movements as I stepped onto the floor and reached for a towel. Water dripped everywhere.

I turned, holding the towel at my side, arching my back a little. "Even right now?"

His eyes roamed my body. Smiled. His eyelashes lowered. "No. I'm not bored now." He batted the water a little.

We had washed together, but we had not done anything else.

I slowly started to dry myself. My bangs had grown since my arrival, and clung to my cheeks. I pushed my wet hair aside with the towel, slowly mopping my body front to back. I knew he was still watching.

The room smelled of sweet-mist, and a little of spice. We had a new liquid soap. Neither of us was sure if we liked it yet.

The air was warm, a little fogged. I liked it as a contrast to the always dry, recycled dome air.

It felt peaceful in here, like an escape to another world. Ari's tone came up and over me, breaking my reverie. "Tahir, you are beautiful."

I think Nik had said that to me once years ago, or maybe I only remembered it that way because I wished it were so.

My reality tilted. Out of place. Out of time. I wanted to be wanted. And with Ari I was. Delegations and moons and kings didn't matter. Only what took place here and now, in this room. This moment.

Seconds later, Ari pressed the lever to drain the pool and stood, water sluicing off him, the liquid flashing against his dark skin. The little plastic starship that had been floating, ignored, to the far side of the pool, tumbled in this new storm.

"Well," I shot back at him, "you look like the god Sinarha himself rising from the void. A water void, that is." I handed him a towel.

He stepped out of the whirlpool, reaching for me. I chuckled and dodged him, going into the alcove that led to the main room. I didn't bother dressing.

Seconds later, he followed me, chasing me through the arch to the bedroom. The curtains hung heavy and velvet, still closed as I had preferred them since yesterday.

I threw my towel on the floor and jumped into a pile of pillows. The lighting had already been set low. There was a fake candle on the wall flickering orangely.

Ari followed, landing next to me, hands reaching for my shoulders. His wet hair fell against my neck and chest as he leaned in to kiss me. I grabbed him around the chest and pulled him to me until our bodies met, and opened my mouth to him.

He tasted of all my pent-up longings exposed. My unchecked desires. My dizziest fantasies. I would never have dreamed this surly man I met in the throne room on my first day would become all of this for me, and more.

We buried ourselves between the pillows, hair still damp, the room air fresh, our skin tingling and cool but beginning the burn of wanting each other until we could not be contained.

I could feel Ari's hitched breathing and rapid pulse against me as I moved in the bed to caress him, first with my hands, then with my mouth. It was never difficult to give him pleasure. Except for hiding his face with his forearm when he came, he had lost much of his initial shyness with me. He was not hesitant to touch me at all now, his hands making me light-headed and hot all at the same time.

The air in the room seemed to become even more moist. Our skin shone even under the shadow of the curtain. We had both found release but my hands still roamed over Ari's chest, down to his groin, keeping him taut and wired.

We rested a little, then made love a second time, slow, ever attentive.

By now Ari's hair had dried. It tangled on the pillow and about his neck. I pushed it back with my hands and combed the soft strands gently with my fingers, moving my body over him, kissing him on the mouth, the jaw, the neck. I noticed the little tugs on his hair made his erection jump against me. He liked when I ran my hands over his head and around it, curling my fingers at his nape. His fingers clung to my biceps, then his arms moved up and embraced me.

I'd only ever done it once, but I wanted him in me again, so I grabbed the oil and rubbed it inside me, and then onto him. I position myself just right, and he stayed still, letting me control. I pushed onto him slowly, controlling every move so it was painless. I adjusted myself to the slip and slide of him and began a rhythm. He gasped out my name. It felt so good, so natural this way, me on top, him inside me. I never wanted it to end.

Ari held me by the hips but didn't push. He just gently rested his hands there. I loved the feel of him sliding into me, the feel of his fingers on my skin lightly caressing, the salty taste of his skin as I kissed and licked his neck. He was so smooth beneath me. I was so aroused I got lost in a kind of daze, a white blankness of pure pleasure, pure Ari. If anyone had ever told me it could be like this, I would never have believed them.

Our bodies fit together so well, as if they'd known each other in secret for a thousand years before we met.

"You are amazing," Ari breathed, hands moving with the barest of touches on my hips and buttocks.

I could only groan in response. He was pure bliss to me. But in the moment, I could not think of the words to say it.

How long it lasted, I couldn't say. We didn't feel the need to rush. I felt the burn of pleasure but never pain. It was great oil we were using, but also Ari was the perfect size for me, perfect in every way. I wanted to tell him. I could feel the gift awakening at this wonder in me, but I kept it off to the side untapped. It wasn't needed. There were no difficulties or problems. No pain. This feeling in both of us was everything we wanted to keep, savor.

My gift was a part of me, but also like an entity itself, curious and alive. It wanted to feel what I felt. It was awake but unmoving, a special light observing, absorbing.

I probably could have healed whole armies right now, and never tired.

Energy moved through me. Surrounding us both.

Ari made a series of deep moans. I, too, was close, hearing myself beginning to cry out. I felt him come inside me at the same time as my own body crested, the moisture spreading between us. I lost air, time, reality. I shuddered in Ari's arms as he gripped me close.

When we caught our breaths, we lay very still, linked. It was only when some time had passed, as we lay breathing in unison, our foreheads touching, that I felt him soften and slip from me.

He said my name softly in the dark.

I kissed him and pulled the pillows and the covers around us.

The shadows of sleep enfolded us. I don't think either one of us stirred until morning.

*

The next morning began a more leisurely day for us. The king did not require Ari until afternoon so we lounged for hours and had breakfast in bed.

When we finally emerged from our rooms, dressed much the same as yesterday, Sullen and the younger escort were waiting. Two more joined them, the four now comprising Ari's and my contingent.

We all headed to lunch.

I had not recently seen the three Darkquill delegates who had insulted me, at least not for many days. Today they were standing very close to the entrance as we came in. We were in the medium-sized banquet room that held barely 100 people. Still a huge chamber to my perspective.

Ari moved forward with an ease associated with living here for the past twenty years. So he did not hear it when one of the delegates said, close to my ear, "Ah, it's the prince with his healer-consort the king paid to bed his virgin son."

I whirled to face the voice, a man this time in a black coat with golden long trains at the arms that unfolded like wings when he lifted his elbows. He was one of the three I recognized from the other day. Before I even knew I was speaking, I heard my voice. "Say that again louder, please, so the king can hear you."

The man just gave me a smile and moved away. The other two, wisely silent, went with him.

I felt a hand on my upper arm from behind. Sullen said softly, "I heard him. Would you like to file a report?"

My face became instantly hot. I moved away from the entrance and to the side of the room. "Is that what people are saying?" I asked him.

"No."

"But some."

"Yes. Some," he admitted.

"Then Ari and Kean know of the gossip."

"I don't know that."

I took a deep breath. I heard that word again in my mind. *Kalalo. You are not wanted.*

"Why would you even offer to file a report for me about what he said? It's not a crime to say what one feels."

"There were three of them. I thought maybe you recognized them from the other night."

"No, those were other people who attacked me. Taller, stronger. But these three had words with me about a week ago. They just don't like me."

"Also, they spoke ill of the prince. Though that's not a crime, Kean would have them sent home early for it. It might make your life more peaceful."

I looked at him thoughtfully for a moment. My pulse had slowed. It had calmed me just to have him near me, talking to me. "Did you get a read on them at all?"

He answered with a half-shrug.

"Tell me," I insisted.

His eyes scanned the room slowly, and came to rest on my face. "A darkness there. A resentment. Maybe even jealousy. I see these things, but I have no context for interpretation most of the time."

"It's a gift you have, you know."

His right eyebrow jerked upward. "Not like yours."

"Yes. Like mine. Just not the same gift."

He smiled gently. "I'm merely one of those who is glad you came here from so faraway. We have been waiting for so long," he paused, then tilted his head, "for life to come back to the king and queen and their son." He blinked twice, as if to brush away a sting.

"Thank you, Sullen. I needed to hear that right about now."

"It's only the truth. You are good for the prince. I can read that."

I wondered if he could read from me how much I loved Ari, even though I had not spoken of it to anyone in those exact words. "If it's not too personal to ask, how do you read the king?"

"I usually keep silent. I don't presume anything, and overstepping another's personal boundaries is not my way. But to you I will say the king is a complicated man. He does nothing for greed, though some people see this current situation as pertaining only to money. He does what he thinks is right and best for the whole and the future. His personal relationships suffer as a result because he does not placate and is a workaholic. The prince feels he is a disappointment in his father's eyes, so there is friction."

I stared at him for a moment. "Thank you for telling me that. It helps me." But I still couldn't forget that Kean had threatened me, that my place here was not secure, as I had been first led to believe.

"There are a lot of things that are strange when you are new to a place. I'm happy to answer your questions as best I can."

"I'll always have questions."

"May I add, I have never seen the prince like this before."

"Like what?"

"Glowing."

"Oh." I gulped.

Sullen gifted me with a half-smile.

I saw Ari motioning me to him. As I moved, Sullen and the second escort moved with me. As we walked, I said to Sullen, "I am glad you're here."

"I do my best to serve," he replied, features schooled to professionalism.

We went to the luncheon table with the king and sat. Winter arrived moments later. She approached Ari and leaned down to him, giving him a loose embrace.

Ari looked both surprised and delighted.

Her near-black hair was folded in elaborate designs, pinned with crystal birds and flowers. She wore a tight-fitting black and green jacket that showed off her narrow waist and figure. You could not tell at a glance that she was middle-aged, at least 90. Only on closer inspection could you see tiny wrinkles at the corners of her eyes, and deeper lines between her eyebrows and at the edges of her mouth. There existed treatments to smooth the skin in those areas, but it seemed she had not had them.

Her presence exuded a formal charisma, like electricity that sparked the air around us. I could feel myself hold my breath as her sleeves nearly brushed mine. We had spoken little, most of it during our meeting right after I had healed Ari. Then, she had been more vulnerable, her emotion for her son showing. But every time I saw her afterward, her regal bearing and almost bored air made her seem unapproachable.

Today, she actually spoke to me, turning from embracing her son. "Tahir, you are looking healthy."

"And you, as well."

Her lashes swept up, long and fake. She wore makeup that looked like gold dust. Her eyebrows threatened her forehead at a severe slant. Nonetheless, she was very beautiful. She and Ari shared the same eyes and chin.

The tails of her dark green coat dragged the floor as she moved to her seat on the other side of Kean. I heard her say to the king, as she was seated, "Why do you avoid my request for meetings?"

"Because you always tell me I spend too much," he calmly replied.

She was queen, but there was no doubt he was in charge. Firm and perhaps even unforgiving. I could not see him otherwise in the past two days, and I swallowed against a bitterness in the back of my throat.

I tried to remember that they had lost five children, all practically still babies. I tried to understand how that might feel, how it would scar the outcome of a long, continuing lifetime until the very day they died and joined their children in the abyss. I had already seen how it had affected Ari apart from the splinter-bomb's effect. Even now I could feel the loneliness in him for Arku to whom he had only recently said his final goodbyes. I know my presence filled a big space inside him. I was happy to do that. He had become so beloved to me.

As I kept pondering these thoughts, the four of us ate mostly in silence, but the rest of the room was a din of chatter, laughter, the hum of lively conversations. As usual, all colors of the spectrum seemed splashed about the room, a combination of decoration, fancy serving ware, and very fine attire. Perfume mixed with aromas of roasted vegetables, meats, and fruit served in dripping syrups. Everything gleamed like new. This was a rich, advanced culture.

One look at the hall and everything in it would tell you all was fine with this realm. At the moment the internal strifes could not be seen or felt.

But I had guards at my back.

And the paperwork that was signed yesterday assured us all now, that the hawkships were being readied, and the mercenaries were coming.

*

That afternoon were more meetings, and more signings and paperwork. Ari looked supremely bored throughout most of it. I couldn't blame him.

During breaks he would come close to me and whisper, "I can't stop thinking about last night."

"Me, too," I replied, trying not to grin.

Feelings are overwhelming when one falls in love. Today, everything looked imbued with golden auras. And when garish clarity reared itself, the instinct was to look away, or laugh, or try immediately to fix it because when you're in love, everything seems that easy.

Today, Ari had taken some of my advice to heart, and either laughed or looked away when it seemed he got too annoyed.

The king's demeanor looked pleased.

I wanted to yell, "I'm not controlling him with my gift." But I focused instead on what I might do to Ari that evening in bed without our many layers of clothes.

Dinner came and went. I was waiting in the hall with Sullen for Ari to make his way out of the banquet room when my necklace chimed. The message was clear and succinct. *Meet me tomorrow at 11. Third floor. Hall A. Bring yourself and your escorts only. Winter.*

I thought about not telling Ari of the message. Just going. But I wasn't going to make the same mistake twice. As soon as he arrived to walk with me back to our rooms, I told him. "Your mother wants a meeting with me."

He nodded. "Everyone's curious about us."

"It's all new to me, too," I told him. "Especially everything being so public, so focused on you."

"I know. It takes some getting used to."

"I'll tell you every word of our conversation. Ari, I don't intend to tell her anything personal. You have my word."

"I know, Tahir. I trust you."

"I wish you were coming with me."

"I didn't get chimed. She wants to see you. Not me."

"You love her very much, don't you?"

"Yes. Don't all sons love their mothers?"

"I don't know. What about their fathers?"

He smirked.

But of course he had to love his father. His father had brought me to him and gone to great lengths to do so, including breaching the net and sending a fleet of ships for me. I would never forget the sight on board the ship breaking through the atmosphere of my home world Alluria to see a flock of giant hummingbirds, all silver, all slowly gyrating in space, sleek and silvery but with a hint of fuchsia and hot green plumage at their sides. Twelve starships including the one that brought me here.

I said, "I've only ever known the man who raised me at the Temple. And I do love him."

"Do you know nothing of your real parents?"

"Zash knows. He told me so. But I never wanted to know, so I never asked him. He respected that and never talked about it."

"How could you never want to know? I think I would."

All I could remember of that day at the Temple entrance was the rain so thick I could not see the yard or anything more than three feet in front of me. Everything so gray and wet in my eyes along with my terrified tears. I understood now why they had left me, or thought I did. For my gift to be best explored, I had to be raised at the Onyx Temple.

"I'm the sort of person who likes to look ahead. Besides, I'm afraid of searching for them."

"Afraid of what?"

"Disappointment."

"Sounds like you already are."

"I was six. I don't remember much."

"But you remember being left behind."

I looked up with a smile.

He took a breath and said, "Well, I hope you don't feel that way here."

At his words my body shivered, part thrill, part awe at his gentle openness, his kindness. A little over two months ago, this man had been ready to kill me. Now he was, in all ways, the one who made me feel most alive.

When we reached our rooms, I turned to say good night to Sullen and the rest of our escorts, thanking them as I always did.

When the door closed, Ari said, "You don't have to thank them every night."

"Of course I do. By the way, did you know Sullen has a gift?"

"A gift for who?"

"No, not that kind of gift. I mean one like mine. He's a reader. He reads emotional states."

"He can tell what I'm thinking?" Ari asked.

"No, he just reads your mood, how you're feeling."

"I'm not sure what good that is as a gift."

"Oh," I said, "it's very valuable. It can calm and sort. It can deal with difficult, out-of-control situations by making those around you feel heard and understood to the core. It can literally save lives. Open communication. With the right kind of training, it could negotiate a gunman to part with his gun. Or a nation to stop a war."

"How do you know that about Sullen?" he asked.

I sensed a tinge of jealousy.

"We just talk." I headed to the counter to make us some tea. "When we're dying of boredom, you know."

I was glad to hear Ari laugh and say, "Yeah, I know."

"The other escorts are so serious. He is, too, but he's more open. I met him the first day I got here. A friendly face in a sea of strangers."

I heard him go off into the bedroom. By the time I was finished making the tea, he came out dressed in his robe, an off-white, calf-length wrap of soft cloth that made his skin look deeply tanned. He took the cup from my hand and sat at the table.

I sat beside him. We checked our screens for news and waves, and picked a vid to watch in bed.

We were a quarter of the way through the vid, lounging comfortably, when our bodies could take no more. We turned it off and tossed the screen on the floor, moving together effortlessly. In the velvet dark, the air grew humid and sweet around us.

14.

Level three was the business floor of the palace, still festively decorated for the holidays, and dotted with elaborate dragon sconces, each one unique, but not as garish as the banquet hall levels, or the king's antechamber, and the throne room.

Winter worked in an oval room with multiple large screens and assistants all around. It was almost like being on the bridge of a starship with herself in command at the center.

When I entered, she looked up and immediately met my gaze.

Her eyes were darker than her son's, her hair gathered back in a single, high tail crowned with pink chiffon and a sparkling of diamonds along the sides. Today she wore not her usual whites, or violets and pale blue silks, but a color that stood between pink and orange. I couldn't name it. It brought to mind a tropical hothouse flower, not fuchsia, not tangerine but something entirely unique. The dress fell in thin waves about her body, gathered with a single-strand beaded belt at the waist.

She wore a fitted, beige bodice over it, along with an earthy pink, knitted scarf over one shoulder. Her fingerless gloves were red. Her leather shoes curled slightly at the toe.

She motioned me to follow her into a more private room, an alcove set up like a lounge, with cushioned sofas, all dark blue, and two tables set with snacks, coffee pots, tea pots, water pitchers. She did not offer me any of it, but told me to sit. The room was well-lit from some hidden source.

I sat on the edge of one couch. She sat on a sofa facing me, also on the edge.

She began without any polite nonsense. "I know the king has requested reports on Arulu. I would like copies."

"Other than at the very beginning, when I healed him, all my reports are verbal," I told her.

Her nod held the stiffness of impatience. "This is typical of him. But I wish to know how my son is faring. In your words, not just the king's."

"Have you asked Ari?"

"I said 'in your words'."

"He is well, Your Highness."

"Call me Winter. Please." It was a polite gesture; there was zero warmth in her tone. "He seems well," she began. "But I used to see him once a day here. Now he doesn't come as often."

"The king has him all day long."

"Yes. He has usurped all of Ari's time." She said nothing of my taking the rest of Ari's time. "When the king focuses on something, he is like that. The dissolving of the net is an obsession with him."

I wished, in that moment, for Sullen's gift of reading. I couldn't tell if she agreed or disagreed with the pronouncement about the net. Surely, as queen, she had had some input.

"You are with him away from his father's demands," she said.

My breath hitched in my throat. I nodded.

"I know the king has ordered you to watch over him, and even use your healing to soften the emotional pain he must still feel."

"Yes."

"Is it that bad?"

What could I say? I promised Ari confidence. Privacy. But his mother seemed honestly concerned.

"A lot has happened to change his life very quickly. His moods can reflect that."

"Yes, but how bad is it? Really?"

"Nightmares, maybe," I replied softly, wondering if even that was going too far.

"Do you take that from him?"

"No. That is not how my gift works. In emotional situations, it can calm and relax, take the edge off so you aren't so— broken." I remembered again when Zash had done that for me when I'd left the Temple, taking my grief into himself so that I could move forward less afraid and more eager. I still recalled the grief, but it didn't choke me.

She sat back. "I see. Strange." She looked at me with clear eyes unmoving, a very strong-willed stare. Then she said, "That is not what the king thinks. He thinks you can help him mold Ari."

"I know."

"Even as a child, Ari was at odds with his father. Defiant. A little spoilt, maybe."

"That isn't an uncommon thing," I said.

"Kean wants a shadow. A copy of himself. He wants a mirror to command and to pass on all his duties to. It isn't realistic." Now she plucked absently at her scarf, but her composure never wavered. "We have argued about this, his father and I."

Winter was the one who had wanted Ari's life ended, compassionately, when his barely surviving body had been found in the ruins of the palace just before Lyric Prime itself was destroyed. But it would have still been murder. I had not spent one moment thinking I might find an ally in her. But now?

"I want him to explore himself, learn to live again," she went on.

I took a deep breath, leaning forward without really thinking about it. But even now my body wanted to listen to her, as well as my mind.

"When this is all over," she continued, "all this pomp and circumstance involving the net, I want you two to go to our private compound on Darkquill. Ari was there a few times as a child, and it's his favorite place, all that is left standing of his childhood memories of places he has lived and loved. All the rest were destroyed. I want you two to live there if you would like it, and learn and grow. Build a life if you wish, or not, but the freedom to make that decision should be there for both of you unhindered by Ari's status in this culture. He needs time to be. I will make his father see this."

"Ari has talked to you about this?" I asked.

"No," she said, lips curving up very slightly.

Ari had mentioned Darkquill to me several times now. Did mothers read minds?

"Tell me, before I make any plans concerning you two after the net is dissolved, if you are even interested in accompanying Ari away from the palace so that he can fully recover himself. If I set it up, would you wish to accompany him to Darkquill?"

This was everything I had tried to ask for Ari from the king. "It would be my honor," I replied. "Ari has mentioned Darkquill to me. But I need to be honest with you. There are some from that moon who have expressed displeasure with me."

"Really? You're not talking about the attack on your person, are you?"

"No. It was more an uncomfortable discussion with strangers."

"Ah, the snobbery of royal politics. It's rampant here. But the delegates of that moon have nothing to do with our private compound there. I want to make plans to offer it to you and Ari, but I needed to understand your wishes, first. And you."

"Understand me?"

She tilted her head. "I can see that my son means something to you. I see him these days and he is different. Even his skin is glowing."

My face heated. She smiled. "You do not need to be embarrassed to take credit where credit is due."

I looked at my hands in my lap, then back up at her.

She said, "Tahir, you intentions appear pure to me. Others may have questions about you, but I do not. You knew nothing of our ways when you came here. You did not know my son or have any agendas other than the command of the king to heal our son. I have watched you interact with my Ari. And I am grateful. He has never had any close friends." Her eyes blinked twice, quicker than normal. I had seen very rare emotion from her at any gathering that wasn't under her complete control. Now her eyes shifted away from me.

I cleared my throat. "I am honored to be his friend. And I can tell you my intentions with him are not casual."

Her smile came slow and remained small, but not hesitant. "Know that if and when you should ever need it, you have my support in this court. And I will talk to the king about all of this shortly."

Her words overwhelmed me. I could barely manage to blurt out, "Thank you."

She rose gracefully from the sofa. I followed. Then she came to me and lightly embraced me, her lips barely brushing my cheek. "Thank *you*, Tahir," she said, backing away.

She led the way out and said formally, "You may return to your tasks of the day now."

I left Hall A and met my escorts in the corridor. I had thought about finding Ari, but lunch was within an hour and I decided to wait until then to see him.

Sullen and the younger guard followed me back to our rooms.

I sat at the table and fiddled with my hand screen for awhile. Bored, I got up and browsed the room looking for something different to occupy myself. There was an ornate, wood cupboard stuffed with some old things of Ari's. I opened it. On one half of one shelf were what looked like old games including an ornate chess set. Also, I saw an old game of worn, wooden tiles. They had been used so much the designs were rubbed off leaving only smears of blue, yellow and red ink. Some old picture books for children, dusty and scratched, made up another whole shelf. A lower level contained a few extra pillows. Yet another, two medium-sized vinyl boxes.

I had never paid attention to those before. Now curious, I wondered what was in them. I told myself to wait until I could ask Ari, but on impulse I bent down and opened the lid of one just to peer in. It was filled with scraps of paper, stacks of all sizes heaping to the sides of the box. I lifted one of the scraps to the edge of the box, bringing it toward the light and saw it was a sketch of one of the dragon sconces in the hall. I picked up another scrap and in the shadows of the closet I could make out the wings of a bird only to realize it was a ship. Next, I grabbed a handful of the papers and brought them into the light, paging through them. There were lots of sketches of the hydroponics gardens. Partial trees. Quick line drawings of people from a distance, no features. And more ships, some rough, some detailed with parts of animals. Lion-ships. Dragonflies. Graceful feminine curves with wings attached to fuselages. Fairy-ships?

Arku had said Ari had tried to design ships with crude drawings even as a child. But these were not the drawings of a youngster, but of someone older. The accumulation looked like many years worth of work.

I heard the door to our room open.

I turned from the open cupboard, some of the drawings still in my hand.

Ari stared at me. When the door shut behind him, he said, "Did my mother tell you to snoop?"

"No. I just now found them. I was bored and opened the doors. I'm sorry, I should have asked first before opening that box." I indicated the two boxes on the bottom shelf.

"These are yours?" I asked.

He came forward, taking them from me and putting them away. "Just when things were really bad and I was waiting for the pain to return with nothing else to do, I'd sometimes draw." He said this casually, as if he were talking about something that was a waste of his time.

"I didn't know you still did it. Arku said you did drawings that showed talent when you were a child. He told me you were a natural. But these are more than that. A lot more."

"Arku might not have known about them—after. If he did, he ignored them. He wasn't always around."

I thought about what I'd just seen. The drawings were intricate, graceful and showing a dedication to the time it would have taken to make them.

Ari added, "I did them when I was medicated. In secret. During the times I felt better."

"Why didn't you show them to anyone?"

"Because they were mine. The only thing I had that I felt was all mine."

"So your father has never seen these? Or your mother?"

"No. And you wouldn't have, either, if you hadn't been snooping."

"I'm sorry."

He shrugged and turned away.

"But, Ari, they really are incredible."

"I don't want to talk about those." He shut the closet hard. "I came because I wanted to hear what my mother had to say to you." He went to the table and sat, placing one leg casually on the chair next to him. His hair fell away from his face and behind his shoulders, gleaming.

I sat across the table facing him. "Your mother is rather amazing for someone who wanted to kill you."

He looked at me with a completely neutral expression. When he said nothing, I continued.

"She wanted to know how you are, of course, but from my point of view."

"What did you tell her?" Mistrust flashed in his eyes.

"I said you were doing well and she agreed. She told me she thought you'd never looked better."

His lips quirked. "She's said that to me, too."

"I didn't tell her anything personal about us. But I thought maybe you had talked to her about going to Darkquill, because she brought that up."

"No. I haven't said a word to her about that. What did she say about it?"

"That she wanted to offer us the compound your family has there. After the net is down, she wants us to go away for a time. A long time, it seems. Enough time to live your own life, explore things a bit."

His eyebrow rose. "She said that?"

"She did. She knows you need time. It's something I tried to bring up with Kean but he wouldn't listen."

He folded his hands over his stomach and stared at them.

"She said she would make sure Kean understands that this is necessary and fair. For you to finally embrace your own life. I'm to go with you if you want me."

He let out an incredulous laugh. "Want you?" He lifted both hands to his face and rubbed at his forehead, talking through them. "How could I not?" It was both a shy and charming gesture.

"But I have duties here," I said. "I'm not sure Kean will easily part with me. And you have duties he wants you to see to every day. It's not going to be easy to convince him to part with you, either. Not after he just got you back."

Ignoring my concerns, he said, "I've been wanting to take you there. It's my favorite moon."

"I know."

His features darkened. "But I'm not going to get my hopes up. My mother has influence, but my father is strict."

"I know. Also, I—I—" I wasn't sure how to phrase my thought. I got up and went to him. I knelt by his knee and reached for both his hands. "I want you to know, Ari, I don't require anything formal. Between us, I mean." I watched the crease between his eyebrows deepen. "I'm willing to go with you for however long you want me, or until you don't want me anymore. No formal attachments necessary."

Ari's chest rose. He lowered his chin and met my eyes. "But I am attached to you, Tahir."

"I know, but it's been so short a time. We don't need to make any complicated decisions. That's all I'm saying. We can take our time. Your mother has great instincts about that, about exactly what we need."

He gripped my hands tightly. "I like the idea of taking our time. And I want you to know I don't want anyone but you."

The smile that rose to my face felt like it turned to a grin. "Me, too." But he still never said it, not in so many words. The actual word *commitment*.

Nor had I. We were both so new at this.

He dropped his leg from the other chair and pulled me up to lean against him, his hands letting go of mine so he could cup my face, steer it to his. He kissed me with a gentle breath. I put my hands on his shoulders and leaned in to deepen it.

When I pulled back, he said, "Tahir, you make me feel like no one ever has."

"I'm glad."

"I wish we could stay here instead of going to lunch."

I frowned, knowing what he wanted, of course, and feeling happy to supply it, but still wondering at that particular shyness in him that caused him to think not much further than our bed. He lived moment to moment as if he did not trust the future, or even want anything to do with that word. But how could he when his biggest experience in life had been to have everything he'd ever loved taken from him within a flash?

"I'd happily skip a meal to spend more time with you," I finally replied.

"But it's a holiday and my father would have a fit."

There was a prolonged moment of head-hanging disappointment. Then we both laughed, our lips meeting again, the kiss long and languid. Ari tasted of warm desire, wistful, yet serene. I felt a slow arousal cover my body. This man could transform me so rapidly with just a touch, make me forget instantly about all the duties we had, all the obligations life was demanding from us.

Right now, I couldn't imagine being without him.

15.

Ari still would not hold my hand in public unless under cover of a table, or pushed into the middle of a large, distracted crowd who were incapable of seeing over each other's shoulders. Yet his shyness did not keep him from wanting to spend time with me. As much time as possible.

On our breaks and sometimes in the early evenings, we took walks together everywhere. Hydroponics. The intersecting pathways around the palace foundation. And longer walks to the moon base and back, over black-flecked, white silt and dust, our leather boots leaving behind their smooth, slightly curving prints.

The sun had risen a few more degrees. A bigger portion of its disk showed over the hills, the coloring of the dome's energy field making it faintly orange. The light was bright enough to dim the moons that followed our orbit, but they could still be seen in the dark blue sky, a trail of lights glimmering off to the south of the sunrise.

As the time grew closer to the day the net would come down, Ari's agitation increased. His moods ran all over, from sullen silence to pent up anger when we were alone in our rooms, and he vented about his continuing frustration with his father.

"Remember," I kept telling him. "Your mother is paving the way for us to go away from here. Only a little more time, that's all we have to endure."

Thoughts of Darkquill kept him in check, mostly obedient during the day. But that wasn't his worry. Having a life. Starting over. No. I could see that didn't concern him. What worried him was much bigger.

Two nights before the appointed date for the dissolution of the net, when all the delegates of all the moons seemed to be holding their breaths now, and talk was more subdued, mealtimes more quiet, he woke me crying out in his sleep. His body trembled in the shadows beside me.

I sat up and thought I saw something make a motion in the room, but it was just a shadow settling at the movement of the curtains when my head had brushed them.

I reached beside me and touched his shoulder which was curved toward his jaw, stiff. He was on his side, hands pressed tight to his chest, his breathing rapid and shallow. More cries came from his throat, choked and garbled. In the dimness I could see the sheet had fallen to his thighs as I had sat up. I could see the outline of the straightness of the waist trailing to his narrow hips. His legs were bent, knees toward his torso, part of the flank exposed. I moved my hand from his shoulder to his back, the skin silken underneath the pads of my fingertips, and began to gently stroke.

"Ari, wake up." I moved my face closer to his. "Ari."

His muscles flexed, jerked, shuddered. I moved my palm over his side, down his arm, along the bare, thin skin of his hip. I slid closer to him, feeling the heat of him, and more tremors. "Ari." Hand on his upper arm, firmer now, I gently shoved to see if that might help him wake faster. His hair was a black pool behind him on the pillow. The paler dark around us seemed to whisper softly.

He cried out again, body jerking, and I slipped one arm underneath him, and continued to call his name.

Finally, his eyes popped open, the whites of them catching the barest of light, glinting. He moaned, and pulled unthinking away from me.

"Ari," I said. "It's a dream. You're awake now."

But I was wrong. He hadn't awakened. He didn't react; he was clearly terrified. He glanced around himself erratically, upper body rising, knees folding into his chest. He was murmuring under his breath. "Stop. Make it stop."

My arm slipped out from under him but my other hand still lay against his shoulder. I gripped it, shaking it. "Ari, you're awake now. It was a dream."

His chest heaved, rising and falling. He was breathing fast now, his eyes still unfocused.

I said his name again. "Do you hear me?" I asked.

But I could tell by his shuttered face he was somewhere else, a place of horror, death, flaying pain. Not our soft bed, the pillows like waves of blue and green. Not our room where the peaceful silence surrounded us. He was nowhere near me, too far from the comfort and the security of a fellow companion who knows his worth.

He kept mumbling, moaning. I thought about turning on a light, but refrained. His turmoil needed to be calmed, not startled.

I continued to speak to him, tone low. "Follow my voice," I repeated a few times. Then said his name again.

The terror in him was a real thing. I could so easily kiss him and, with the gift, take that terror into me and dissipate it. It would be like breathing to me. Like picking up a sharp object and discarding it in the trash. But he had forbidden it.

I knew the nearness of the impending day of the net coming down was causing this, creating echoes within him of the splinter-bomb, memories frothing to the surface of the violent and gruesome deaths of his brother and sisters, their bodies torn, ravaged, their blood painting the leftover debris in gouts of red. I'd seen it all in his mind when I healed him. The visions of his suffering still prickled an abject horror within me.

He wasn't calming.

It took many minutes before he would even allow my embrace without pushing me away. His murmuring eventually gave way to quiet, hitched breaths. His damp cheek pressed my chest.

I was agitated. I wanted to give him the kiss more than ever. The instinct flooded me. My gift felt like a wave in my mind, ready to crest but not allowed to do so. My blood sped through my veins with untapped energies. A bitterness coated the back of my mouth.

My hands went automatically to his face, cupping it, lifting it up. I could see the glimmer of moisture on his cheeks, feel my palms slide against them. My head bowed. My mouth parted the tiniest fraction.

Ari blinked, then said my name. "Tahir."

I heard it a second time. "Tahir."

That forlorn voice triggered the energy within me even more; it was like the biggest, deepest wind trying to escape and there was nothing left for me to hang onto. The muscles in my hands tightened against his face. My head bent.

Where does the darkness go when it is tired of being chased by the light? Into itself. Where does the heart open with true desperate longing like a child's hand reaching for the unknown? Inside the core of all that we are as defined by the abyss from which we came.

I couldn't bear it, his pain even though he seemed to be calming, and before I knew what was happening I touched my lips to his, gentle, warm, chaste. The gift woke completely. It was instinct alone that roused it, along with my inability to merely watch and accept a being in such agony.

I took into myself the edges of his devastation, breathing in the smoky tendrils, smoothing the acid bumps, the hidden pockets of salt and teardrop, the silently raving, still-bleeding wound of Arku that hovered over all the newer hurts.

I did not forget my promise to Ari to never touch his emotions. I simply broke it. I couldn't control it anymore, and my gift lashed out, obedient to my out-of-control nature.

Ari's lips opened to me, but only because he was pliant for the moment. Exhausted and still half asleep. His long hair fell across his face; it tangled with my kiss, but I didn't care.

I held him close, tight. My gift welled up even stronger, an oceanic curve of depth knowing no bottom, endless. It climbed up my insides and through my mind. I saw it as a rushing tide, arcs of gold, prisms of light. The frothy crest of it encircled a bent silhouette, a man standing against a backdrop of ceaseless red scarred with slashes of ever-moving black. Ari raging. Ari weeping. My gift surrounded him in that awful mental space that stabbed and stabbed at him, at *us*.

It touched the top of his dark head. A blue-ness entered me. Ari. Essence of harrowing flame, ash, electric blue, hot blue, driven blue so compressed its center was pure white.

My Ari burning. I would not have it!

As my gift advanced, closing the circle to touch him, I saw him anew, half shadow, half rising sun, heir to the Realm and offspring of pain. Brother. Son. Lover. Prince. Ari was as striking as the god Sinarha who came from the abyss and took away the memory of immortality from all human life in the galaxy. This was the third time I'd see him as an image of that god. A large piece of that darkness had formed him, was a part of him, and my kiss veered toward it.

I could feel Ari tugging at me now, the fight in him returning, his lips against mine crushing as he tried to push against me. Unthinking, my hands held him firm when he tried to pull away.

The gift rushed at him with light. With the glitter of tears turned to sweet rain, the warmth of nebulas melting into our skins. I brought with me flushed, orange breezes scented with green leaves and twilight, the verandas of summer, the falling stars that spell out our childhood wishes.

I met ice and hail. A voice came from within, dark and heavy, adorned with tears and pins and giant knives. It threw me back. "Stop!" It made me confused. "Tahir!" It wrenched my heart. "Stop!"

I tried to take a deep breath. Couldn't. Hands pressed my chest. Lips sucked at teeth that seemed to bite. A swirl of storm. A cold and frigid backlash.

In the bed I felt myself jerk back. This had never happened to me before. But then, in all my healings throughout my life, either the person had been unconscious, or I had had permission even if the patient's mind was permeated by fear and mistrust.

Light from under the curtains edged the dark. Ari's silhouette, in waking reality, was staring at me. My body swayed.

I realized what I had done. I was breathing thinly, hands at my lap now. Ari still had both of his pressed hard against my chest, palms up and holding me back.

"I'm sorry." My voice came as if from a long distance, stuttered with shock and the sting of being thrown back so harshly and darkly into myself. I was still reeling.

I could hear Ari's breaths coming loud and fast. "What happened?" he asked; there was tenseness there, and not a little anger.

My voice came in a low rush. "I wanted to help. I couldn't stop myself."

In disbelief, Ari said, "But you have been helping me. Every day." His head moved, tilting. "You've been making me stronger. In the ways that count."

"I—I—" But I lost the thought and my voice.

"But not like this." He said it softly. Then again. Harsh. "Not like this!"

I sat very still and tried to think, to examine what had just happened. And why.

"You haven't done this before, have you? While I was sleeping maybe?"

My heart stabbed. "No. Never!"

"You promised me." Now the way his voice angled over me, I felt the accusation and the fury.

"I did promise. And I meant my promise. This is the first time. It just came over me." I was still trying to figure it out. The way the wave of the gift had crested as if having gone beyond my will and asserting itself. An instinct uncontrolled.

"Then, I don't understand."

I lowered my head. "I'm not sure I do, either." I tried to reach for his hand. He pulled away. Desperately, I said, "I didn't mean to do it!"

His breaths came short; he was still shaking.

I looked around, reorienting myself, seeing the walls, the velvet curtains, the bed, the alcove beyond which led to one door to the bathroom, one to the kitchen area. I saw the shine of the hard floor marred by the square of a soft, dark rug.

Ari was still staring at me in disbelief.

I said, "The connection didn't complete. Nothing touched you."

"Because I pushed you off me."

I winced at the truth. "I'm so sorry." This was unconscionable. I didn't understand myself. "Ari, I mean it. I'm so sorry."

I reached for his hand again but he pulled it away.

He said, voice held under shaky control, "I don't remember everything. Was I suffering so much?"

"Your nightmare?"

"Was that it?"

"I guess. I don't know."

"I've had them before. What was different this time?" As if in answer to his own question, he drew a hand furiously across his face, wiping at the moisture there.

"You wouldn't wake up. And when you did, you weren't hearing me. You weren't seeing me."

He crossed his arms tightly across his abdomen, sitting on the edge of the bed, knees bent. I was facing him, my back against the wall. The edge of the curtain brushed my hair. "But still, why that---kiss. You kiss me all the time and you don't use the gift."

"It just came over me. Took over."

I heard him take a deep breath.

"Ari, please forgive me."

"I do. I believe you. But I still don't understand."

A hot relief flooded me.

He continued. "I thought you had to prepare beforehand. I thought it was all a conscious act."

"It is. But I care for you so deeply that something inside me sort of broke open, I guess. It was as if I had endless energy. I couldn't not respond to your pain."

"Then this could happen again?"

"I won't allow it. I swear it took me off-guard." I reached for him a third time. He allowed my palm to touch the top of his hand but did not move to return the touch. He was still shivering, imperceptible to the eye now, but I felt it through the skin.

"So you just acted without thinking." He was struggling to understand this as much as I was.

I nodded. "I remembered my promise just before the gift started to take your pain." I didn't tell him that for a moment there, as the gift crested, I didn't care about that promise. "I pulled back."

Finally, he leaned back into the pillows, his hand sliding away from mine and going to pull up the sheet. I reclined alongside him, reaching for a light blanket as well. We did not touch.

We both stared into the dark. Finally, Ari said, "It's a big day tomorrow. The final day we live under the net. Lots of stupid ritual. I have to be dressed up and ready to go by 7."

"I know."

"We both need to sleep."

"I know."

"I'm sorry I woke you."

"You don't need to be sorry, Ari." It was I who felt the need to apologize. Again and again.

He did not reply.

I turned onto my side, hoping he would respond and face me. Instead, he turned his back to me and pulled the sheet closer to his head. I grasped a pillow instead, and closed my eyes.

16.

Ari had barely spoken to me all morning. He'd rushed through dressing and left our room without a glance back to see that I followed, which of course I did.

At lunch he was polite but quiet. I'd seen him fume over a small triviality with his father once earlier in the day. I never found out what it was about.

I heard fragments of statements from all different voices throughout the banquet hall. People were mingling after lunch, and through the din floated random opinions.

"...people are staying home from their jobs tomorrow..."

"...not enough time to prepare..."

"...twenty years too long..."

"...trading peace for strangers with guns..."

"...threaten to move outside the Realm..."

"...our wealth secured by commissions for starships by the thousands..."

On and on it went. People listing the pros and cons of the king and his council's decision. The anxiety level was red-lined, an engine heating too fast to contain. The flames were high.

Amidst all the gilt and luxury of the room, gold flashes of dragon-light and fake flame, bowls of bubbling founts of purple wine, people festooned with the colors of auroras and preening like peacocks, I saw Ari shadowing his father. The tension in

Ari's body was obvious to me, but he held himself still, kept his chin high.

Last night I had seen inside him for the first time since the healing. His storms, his sadnesses and insecurities, his barely held-back resentments and fears, but also an iron will. He might be muddied, mired and scarred, but it was who he was. That iron will had come from his suffering. It amazed me.

Sometimes I forgot my Temple lessons. One wisdom often brushed aside by so many students: *In varying light, weaknesses can also be strengths.*

I sat at one of the empty tables and poured myself more wine, then leaned on my upturned hand and watched him through bleary resignation.

I had fucked up.

At this most transforming of times for his entire Realm, now who could he trust?

I felt Sullen at my back in silent support. I moved my hand up from my chin to my forehead and rubbed.

Finally I turned to him. "Sullen."

"Yes?"

"You'll be there tomorrow?"

"Yes."

"I can't wait for it all to be over."

He nodded, but did not smile.

*

The conference room, another large area off the throne room much like the king's antechamber, had mostly emptied.

The walls were white; it made the room seem bigger because the ceiling was so tall. Beautiful columns of black marble lined one side, which was decorated with fringe-handled, decorative swords. Mostly, the room was made up of seating arrangements for meetings, two long tables of black wood facing each other with a space in the middle, and one round table at the back for smaller, more intimate gatherings.

The entire ceiling had a pale night sky painted on it, full of stars and dragonships and ships with trees for masts and ships with swan necks and ships like city skylines.

I was still sitting toward the end of one table, near the back of the room. Ari was seated near the end of the other table. He looked up and met my eyes. Unsmiling. All in red again, as he would be tomorrow for the big event, his sleeves trimmed in silver dragged across the tabletop as he leaned on his forearm. I couldn't read him but he was darker-eyed than usual, brows narrowed.

My heart jumped once in my chest. My eyes heated because his look was so closed. I crossed my arms and leaned against the back of my chair.

Voices came in from the hall, discussing the organization of tomorrow's ceremony. It was to be at the landing field of the moon base. Ten hawkships would descend, one for each moon, and land to form a circle about the official proceedings. Computers were programmed to dismantle the net at the stroke of a key on the king's command.

So much to think about and still to do. Already the landing field was being readied by workers.

It was now late afternoon. Gray light through rectangle windows on one side of the conference room striped Ari's hair making him look older. His mouth was a thin line. Finally, he swept up his thin viewscreen, curling his fingers about the edge, and rose, looking away. He made his way to the exit as if he had never even seen me.

My chest constricted.

"Sullen?" I said, without turning.

Before I could form more of a question, he replied, "Today is a hard day for a lot of people. You are here for him and that is what matters."

I took a deep breath and stood, following Ari and the rest of the royal contingent into the hall and to the throne room for the final meeting before dinner. I felt Sullen close behind, but it was no comfort.

*

The king made a speech all about trust and risk, safety and fear. There was discourse about commerce and industry, and the greatness of the artisans of the Realm of the September Stars. He was recorded by dozens of holos. This was one of three speeches he would give between today and tomorrow.

Standing against a wall near the front sidelines, I tried to listen to it. Concentrate. But all I could hear was the whir of floating technology, recording devices, the breathing of the audience, the rustling of satin against leather against velvet. There were lines of benches where most were seated, but many stood, filling the huge throne room to the edges of its carven walls. Rich colognes filled the air trying to hide the nerves of a perspiring court and nine delegations.

Ari stood, a streamlined, red figure, to the left of the king. Winter stood to the king's right. She had as much a right as queen to make her own speech, but Kean's introduction made clear the speech was united and from both of them, and that through personal agreement he would be the speaker.

I heard about every third word. My eyes kept going to Ari, who had mostly continued to ignore me today. I kept asking myself why I thought I was losing my heart, then telling myself I was being stupid. This was a tiff about a small transgression in the night. We were both still so new to this. Relationships. Living together. Sleeping together.

I kept playing our conversation over in my mind. *"Then this could happen again?"* he had asked.

And I wondered about that. I had told him I wouldn't allow it. But I had allowed it. I had blindly reached for him, my empathy completely out of control. How did I know I would be able to keep my promise in the future?

But I did know. I wouldn't do anything like it again. Not unless he consented. I would not touch him. I would wait. I would wait forever for him in any regard if it came to that.

145

Sullen touched me on the shoulder. I jerked my head up, not expecting it.

With a nod of his head, he motioned me out of the room. I did not want to leave Ari, but Sullen seemed intent. We were close to the front. I knew Ari would see me leave. He would not be able to miss me all in black, flanked by two escorts. He'd wonder where I was going and why. I hoped it did nothing to disrupt his control.

The corridor beyond the throne room was wider than on the other floors, and led to many exits and doors and alcoves that overlooked the moon base, the sunrise, the city of Xia. It was empty except for pairs of guards at each door, and one or two people conferring animatedly on jeweled communicators. The landing to the staircase was closest to us. Sullen and his partner led me directly to it, and ascended a short curve with me following.

I heard the heavy breathing before I saw him. A fallen man, his leg twisted under him, his face frozen as if trying not to cry out in pain.

"The medics were called but they are slow to arrive," Sullen said, kneeling at the man's side.

I went to him immediately. "I can heal him now," I said. "With minimal shock to his system," I added. "The medics would have to move him to treat him."

A broken leg took little preparation on my end. I would feel nothing but an ache for a moment, and then fatigue.

I knelt on the step below the fallen man, directly in front of Sullen, and took the man's face in my hands. He was dark-haired, the longer ends braided like so many, and had light brown eyes. He could have been anywhere between 50 and 80, younger than Kean, but much older than me and Ari.

"I can take your pain," I said, as I felt all my instincts awaken. Just as it had been last night, the gift was ready. In fact, it was more than ready, still highly energized because it had not expended itself to completion with Ari.

His face was reddened, shining with pain-sweat. He nodded. His body shook as if cold. He wore deep purple and pink scarves braided about him. I wondered if one of those scarves had tripped him. The mix of modern with old-fashioned apparel had many layers and much of it was not meant for long walks, or gently spiraling staircases.

"What's your name?" I asked.

"Daygen."

His lips were gray. I could tell he was already in shock. The situation was dangerous and still without medics on the scene.

"Don't be alarmed, Daygen. It is a touch of lips, nothing more. You will be fine, as if it never happened."

His eyes widened but he did not protest. He was suffering too much. "How long?"

"But a moment to your mind." I lightly caressed his hair with one hand to soothe.

He shut his eyes and said, "Do it."

I bent and my lips met his. The gift soared. It curled about him and into his mind. His lips trembled against mine. I saw him standing on a white field and my gift, like a cloud of golden lights, descended upon him. I saw the lights go directly to his leg, encircling it. Then I was inside him as well, my essence, my thought, feeling the twist of bone, the rapidness of his heartbeat, the clamminess of his skin. The ache of the bone came over me like a hollowness, then rapidly receded, floating around me like a cloud being systematically dissolved by wind.

The bone itself began to mend, cracks sealing, strength and wholeness returning. Swiftly, it was done.

I pulled my head back and let go of his face. A moment of dizziness rushed me. I felt hands on my shoulders. Sullen.

Daygen sat up. Then stood. "That's incredible! I feel fine. My leg is fine." He bounced on it a little to test it.

I stood slowly, Sullen supporting at my elbow, and smiled. "It is my honor to have healed you."

He looked at me then. "I've seen you around. Heard about you. I thought it was amazing that the prince had recovered, but

I didn't really believe it was that simple. The talent of one healer, one man. You are Tahir?"

"Yes."

"I have seen you at banquets eating with the royal family. But I still wasn't sure what to believe. Thank you."

"You are most welcome."

"If you ever find yourself on Snoglobe, you have an open invitation to my home, a beautiful estate, actually. In what are called the Impresario Mountains. Daygen Kienkan. I am easy to find."

I nodded.

He said, "How may I repay you?"

"I am paid already," I said.

He took off a gold ring and held it out to me. "At least take this. It's rubicite. It glows pink and yellow in the light."

"No," I said. "You needn't pay me."

"But I would like you to have it."

"Because he has offered twice, to not take it now would be an insult," Sullen said softly from behind.

I felt a little nauseated. I held out my hand. The ring nestled in my palm and I closed my fingers over it. It was warm. It felt old.

"I'm tired," I said to Sullen.

A hover was arriving with the medics just then. They came to Daygen, surrounded him and asked him questions. But he was fine now and I turned away. Another hover came, and Sullen and my second escort boarded, taking me up to the royal level. We floated down the hall to my and Ari's rooms. I was grateful not to have to walk all that way.

I entered the room, left the gold ring on the table, and grabbed a glass of water on the way to the bed. I drank half of it, then lay back against the cool pillows in the shadows of our bedroom.

I gripped my necklace and chimed Ari. It went straight to "hold."

After that, sleep took me in a swirl as it always did after any healing. I'd be fine in probably less than an hour.

When I woke my necklace was singing. Confused for a moment, I had to look around me to remember where I was.

I looked at the tiny screen. *You're missing dinner.*

I messaged Ari back. *I meant to chime you but fell asleep after healing a broken leg on the stairway.*

Words sang back to me. *We all heard about that.*

Good.

Are you going to join us for dessert?

Give me five minutes.

I'll see you.

Now that I was reoriented and had slept, I was fine. I'd slept a surprising two hours. My clothes were wrinkle free, but I sprayed some scent on myself, washed my face and combed my hair.

I came into the hall to find Sullen still out there. The guards never left, of course, but it seemed he himself never took a break.

"I'm informed I still have time to make dessert," I said. "By the way, when do *you* eat?"

He just smiled at me.

17.

When I came into the sparkling banquet hall, few people noticed, most in heavy conversation, drinking, laughing, arguing, eating.

I took my empty place next to Ari on the outside of the royal table. The king and queen glanced up and nodded. Ari looked at me sidelong. "Been playing hero again?"

His words would have caused me to smile at any other time. But after last night they made me unsure, self-conscious. I merely looked at him, let out a breath, and then raised my hand to the wine. The way the light hit it tonight, it was dark, almost black.

Kean said, "Welcome, Tahir."

Winter said, "Tahir, hello."

Beside me, Ari picked at his chocolate mousse, spoon dinging against the parfait glass, but he did not eat.

I was thirsty and hungry. I downed half a glass of wine, and finished the dessert in minutes, looking around for more.

Ari knew I got hungry after healings. He pushed a plate of freshly iced cookies my way.

"Thank you."

"Eat," was all he said.

There was tea and I had some of that. And some kind of leftover bread to my right that had not yet been taken away. The bread turned out to be tasty rolls stuffed with meat, and I ate them as well.

When I was done eating, I drank more wine, two or three more glasses to assuage the discomfort I still felt from Ari. The wine relaxed me. My muscles became more fluid and I didn't mind my thoughts so much anymore about Ari, about the next day's big festivities, or about being *kalalo* in the wealthy and beautiful and gifted Realm of the September Stars.

Ari still said nothing to me. I wanted to speak, but couldn't think of anything to say. I looked out over the hall. I saw a man at a far table wave his hand at me. Daygen.

I nodded at him.

Just then, the king made a toast and everyone had to stand. I didn't mind more drinking. It was doing me good. But standing brought nausea. I'd eaten too quickly. Drank too fast. I swayed.

The hand that caught my shoulder was not Ari's. Sullen kept me from falling. Ari simply looked at me, then at Sullen. He laughed hollowly. I had no idea what to make of it. I couldn't wait for this night to be over.

When the toast, which was rather long and rambling, and which I heard none of, finally ended, Ari turned to Sullen. He put a hand on my arm and said, "I got him."

Then I felt myself being led off the dais and through the curtains to the more private royal exits. Our escorts followed.

Ari said quietly, "I hope you got enough to eat."

"I came in time for the sweets. I love sweets." I realized I truly was drunk, because I laughed as I spoke, as if every chosen word were funny. "But I might have to throw them up," I added.

"Come on," he said, with a hint of annoyance, pulling me along.

I wasn't sure why he was annoyed at me. I'd done well today. I'd bothered him very little, and I'd healed a man in shock from a broken leg. But I didn't ask. I figured his temper would wane eventually. My beautiful Ari. My prince. How could he stay mad at me? Besides, nothing had happened last night. The gift had not completed its touch upon him. I'd pulled back before it did. I'd done everything I could to make the situation right.

When we got to our suite, I found myself needing to sit again. I sprawled into a cushioned chair by our kitchen table.

Ari stood with his arms crossed, halfway into the kitchen area, looking at me. "I'll make coffee," he finally said, and turned away.

I'd drunk the purple wine heavily other nights, and he never looked at me like that. Surly. Disapproving.

I said, "Tomorrow's going to be a hard day. How much wine did you have?"

He didn't answer.

I leaned forward, crossing my arms over the tabletop and put my head down on them. I thought, *He can't be mad at me, Why is he mad at me?* In my drunken mind, it just didn't seem fair.

I think I slept for a minute. I jerked awake from the smell of coffee, and lifted my head.

Ari set the blue, flower-painted cup by my head. Steam rose in sleepy curls. The aroma was faintly vanilla with a bitter, sharp edge.

I straightened and put my hands around the hot cup.

Ari was still standing, his own cup in hand. Even after a long day, he looked fresh. Beautiful. He was staring at the table, and at the ring I'd thrown there earlier in the afternoon.

"What's that?" he asked.

"Payment."

"For the healing?"

"Yeah. I didn't want to take it but Sullen said it would be an insult after the patient offered twice."

"That's protocol here." He frowned. "And idiotic, too." His words came out cold.

"How much do you think it's worth?" I asked.

He shook his head and sat, looking confused. "A hell of a lot."

"Really?"

"Thousands."

"It means nothing to me."

He shrugged. "You should wear it. It's pretty. Or keep it for the future."

"What do you mean 'for the future'?"

"If you ever find yourself adrift, at least you'll have money."

Adrift. Alone. Away from here. That was what he meant. My heart skipped a beat.

I said, trying not to pout. "I spend nothing living here. Your father is generous. Even after a little over two months, I have a lot."

Ari picked up his cup and took a quick sip. Through the steam, his eyes found me. He said, "With that ring you have even more now."

I watched him put the cup down and stare at it. His hair spread over both shoulders, darker today, holding less light within its strands. He wore red nearly every day now. I loved him in red. His face was smooth, beautiful despite the distance in his eyes.

I sighed, saying, "I'm not going anywhere, at least not by my own will." My voice lowered and came out sounding almost wet. "I don't want to." I took my first sip of the hot brew. It was excellent.

"We both have a lot of things we don't want to do," he said.

I looked up, blinking. "I don't know what that means, what you just said."

He glanced away.

"Ari?"

He didn't move.

"Why are you--?" I took a breath. "Nothing happened last night. But you're still punishing me."

He opened his mouth, eyes now downcast. I thought he was going to say something. He remained silent.

"I'm on your side, Ari," I nearly whispered. I was sobering quickly, and not from one sip of coffee.

"I know. What I said came out wrong. I just can't—I can't deal with so much right now. It's hard to concentrate. One thing at a time. Even making coffee was hard." He almost smiled. The expression was diminished when he said, "And then you get drunk like this. Again. One more thing to deal with."

"I'm not drunk. Not now. I ate too fast and I wanted to throw up. But not because of the wine. So make of that what you will." He was deliberately mixing everything up. Because of him I was happy. Because of him I was enjoying myself of what few pleasures I could discover outside of our bed.

"And Sullen—" he began.

"What about Sullen?"

"He just—must like your smell or something. He stands too close."

"What?"

"Well, that came out wrong, too." He scowled. "Just something I sense."

"I have few friends here." I sucked hard at my teeth, trying not to make a face.

After he made no response, I added, "Are you jealous?"

He smiled, but it was one I'd seen on him before I'd healed him, not nice at all.

I tipped my face into my upturned palm. "Well, you shouldn't be."

I never recalled in my days at the Temple being overly sensitive, quick to temper. But this man brought it out in me. I could feel it building, tension, disbelief, impatience, and all residing in me. New to me. Unsettling me.

My stomach ground against itself. "I think he has kids, you know."

"Who?"

"Sullen."

"So?" Ari said.

He was really pushing it.

"Why are you so angry at me? I'm on your side." I kept making that statement today, but it seemed to be getting me nowhere.

"You work for my father. Tell me it isn't true that what happened last night didn't have anything to do with his orders. Not even one thought!"

I looked directly at him but he wouldn't meet my eyes. "It didn't."

His eyelashes fluttered. "No?"

"No. It was something in me about my feelings toward you. Deeper. Different from anything I've ever felt."

Now he looked at me with a more tender expression. "Different like how?"

My body stiffened. My heart beat hard in my throat. How could I say that his pain and sadness made me feel sad? That I felt like I was coming apart? That I was falling in—

"I don't know." I was a coward. I didn't even try to find the words. Or word.

"But you said 'different'. Is that a good thing or bad?"

154

"Good." I got up then, leaving the coffee. I looked at him sitting there, a coil of boiling energy, a prince who did not want to be a prince, who was so unhappy. And scared.

I told myself he was mad at me because he was mad at himself. Because he was still a child who couldn't deal very well with real emotion yet, beyond pain and suffering and enduring it all.

This wasn't about drinking too much purple wine. This wasn't about Sullen. He wasn't afraid of me, or broken promises. It was about tomorrow and the exposure of the Realm.

But there was one other thing, too, that we were both afraid of. It was in the air around us since my meeting with Kean. His father could send me away. At any time I could be banished.

And then what would Ari do?

"I'm going for a bath. Care to join me?"

"No. I can't. I have stuff to do. I need to try to concentrate right now." He reached for his thin, silver reading screen.

"All right." But I walked toward him, lifting my hand and brushing it lightly over his shoulder. "Ari," I said softly, "after tomorrow everything will be better. I promise. We just have to get through it."

Slowly, he nodded.

In the bath, I hoped he would change his mind, take a break and join me. I waited longer than I normally would, prolonging the bath. He never came into the room.

When I came out in my robe he was still sitting at the table and manipulating diagrams on his screen.

I went to bed early and read until I fell asleep.

Some time in the night I woke and felt his warmth in the bed beside me. Asleep. Or maybe pretending to be asleep but really wide awake, trying not to disturb me. Or to dream.

I brushed my fingers against the heat of his arm. He remained still and quiet. I moved my fingers down a few inches and wove them with his. I waited a long time. He never moved.

Eventually, I fell back to sleep.

18.

Ari had opened one side of the curtains over the bed before I was even awake. The silvering light of a seemingly endless dawn disrupted my sleep. Which was why I'd closed them in the first place.

"Close that, please," I said.

"You have to get up," he replied, leaving the curtain half-open. "We have half an hour before we're to meet my father for breakfast. Then on to the landing field."

I sat up, the covers falling away. Ari was wearing lightweight, white sleep pants. I wore nothing, as had been my habit every night since moving in with him. I watched him glance at me, then turn away.

"Are you all right?"

"No," he answered quickly, and walked into the dressing room.

I put on my robe and went into the bathroom.

We left for breakfast together having barely spoken a word. I knew Ari was nervous. He hadn't slept well, if at all. I could tell by the telltale redness around the rims of his eyes.

The future---his future—was coming too fast.

If only we both could just make it through the day.

Today Ari wore a red suit without too many scarves, just the one silver scarf draped over his left shoulder. Silver buttons fitted it to his waist down each side. I'd never seen it before. He had one silver scarf draped over his left shoulder. Underneath the fitted jacket he wore a white blouse that zipped tightly at the throat. The tails of the red coat met at the insides of his knees. The streamlined effect made him look taller and more slender than ever. Just to look at him sent flutters through my diaphragm.

My only comfort for the coming day was that I saw him noticing me, too. I decided to wear more color. No black. My jacket was of pale satin, blue like the clearest, tropical sea. My shirt and trousers were gray. I caught a glimpse in a small, round mirror by the door on the way out and didn't recognize myself.

By midmorning, the net would be down. People were calling it Net Destruction Day under their breaths.

The king made another speech before breakfast. He referred to this day as the Return of the Stars, with no mention of the more negative euphemism with the word "destruction" in it, and in his speech he made sure to say 'Return of the Stars' about twenty times in the five minutes it took him to say words like "welcome to the future" and "auspicious occasion" and "for the good of the Realm." When he finished, there was applause. He was a good leader. His tone and his words filled the room. He had the kind of charisma people could not look away from, and a friendliness about him that people believed in. Even I believed, despite having given my heart to Ari.

After that speech, I wasn't sure if my anxiety was my own, or just me mirroring Ari.

Ari kept himself perfectly in check, but his body was stiffer than I'd ever seen it. He drank some tea and ate maybe one spoonful of eggs. That was it.

I also was not hungry. But I forced myself to eat, tasting none of it. Everything was polite, fake, polished to a gleam as if to reassure everyone perfection meant security. That if everything was in order, nothing could go wrong.

Most of the guests seemed willing to believe. There had been dissent, but today they were more animated than yesterday, accepting the change, looking forward to what it would bring. I did not overhear anymore naysayers. I saw the Darkquill contingent eating together at one table, and none of them looked particularly glum, not even my three personal bullies.

Ari sat beside me, aloof as a December day on my home world of Alluria. I wanted to tell him that everything would be all right. With hawkships and mercenaries and security details, he would be fine. Nothing would harm him. This was not like his childhood.

I wanted to hold him close to me, not caring if everyone saw. I wanted to say I was not going anywhere, no matter what anyone commanded of me, and I would never let him go, we would stay together and be stronger for it. But most of all, I wanted to prove to him he could trust me.

When I thought that, a tiny flame of anger burned inside me. My mind kept telling me nothing had happened when my empathy had taken over. Ari wasn't being fair by closing me out. But today was so hard. We both had too much on our minds.

After today, we would have time for each other. We would be all right. I comforted myself with those thoughts.

After breakfast we all filed out of the large hall and slowly filled the waiting hover crafts. The ceremony was in two hours, but all of us needed time to get there, to mingle, to take our final places.

The royal family, the immediate council members, me and all our escorts waited in the private halls to board last. We would be the final arrivals to make the grand entrance that was expected at the moon base.

Sullen was there, and the usual faces of Ari's most trusted escorts as well.

I had a few spare moments to watch Ari, to see if he noticed Sullen, or had any reaction to him being there. He did not. In fact, he seemed to overlook him entirely.

Sullen had said nothing but a greeting to me today. He was intuitive about such things as what Ari and I were going through, which was a part of his own special gift, like mine and yet so different. But he remained quiet.

There were about three dozen of us waiting for the final hover, the royal one with railings that were draped with red velvet and gold fringe. The same one with the benches in the center that had brought me to this palace on my arrival nearly ten weeks ago.

I leaned in to Ari and said softly, "I feel like I'm coming full circle."

"We all do," was his toneless reply.

I reached out and brushed his hand. His shoulders tightened. But he turned to look at me, finally, and added, "I'm glad you're here."

It was as if my heart had stopped for a day, and suddenly started again. The current of my blood flowed freely once more. My body tingled.

Just then a guard spoke loudly to the entire group. "We're ready for the boarding of the royal craft."

The order had been arranged. The courtiers and their escorts boarded first. The immediate family, with me, boarded last. I still felt out of place, but I was with Ari and that was where I needed, and wanted, to be.

Nerves all around caused people to talk excitedly, then become immediately still.

When we finally boarded, Ari took care to see I was beside him, which made me feel wanted again. He touched my forearm, pulling me close as we both stood at the edge where the gate was shut behind us.

The hover moved silently, its propulsion system completely invisible. A pilot dressed in a black suit, her hair like a big bow, controlled it remotely from a small handscreen. She wore ten round bracelets on her wrist that jingled together in the thin air. Other than that, and occasional soft, nervous chatter, it was the only sound.

As we approached the moon base landing field, I could smell the leftover exhaust from the ships that had landed early in the morning. The scent was like nothing I'd ever experienced before coming here. There was no burnt smell, or ozone, but more of a sweet depth of campfires, and faint tangerine.

Now the field was closed for the ceremony. Only the ten hawkships would be allowed to land. They were not yet here.

The field had been turned into a temporary amphitheatre. There was a floating stage surrounded by green plants in beautiful, painted pots. Blue banners with fields of stars flew as if suspended by nothing.

Ari and I were the first ones to disembark onto the scratchy, dark surface of the field. The sun was east of us, the stage south so people wouldn't have to squint to see. All the weird, gray light made everything grainy and unreal.

Music came from somewhere unseen, strange and alien to me, and a lot of people had already arrived, more than were at the breakfast in the banquet hall. Hovering holocams were everywhere and more guards than I'd ever seen. The field was mobbed with color. Flickering landing lights floated overhead.

I accompanied Ari from person to person, group to group, as he made polite conversation. Most of the people ignored me, but I did see Daygen again, and he greeted me, then thanked me for his healing two more times.

When he left, Ari said, "He's the one who gave you the ring?"

"Yes."

I never left Ari's side, nor he mine. We had little time to converse alone, but there were occasional minutes. During one of those moments, he said, "It's easier now that it's all done and we're standing here."

"Yeah. The build up has been stressful. After everything your people have been through, this is quite momentous."

"I feel like I can breathe again."

"Me, too."

He smiled. "Even though I am opposed to my father's decision, at least it's all almost over. I barely slept," he added softly.

I sighed. "Me, either."

160

"Sorry I opened the curtains into your eyes this morning."

I grinned quickly. "Apology accepted."

Only a half an hour to go now.

Refreshments, mostly various sorts of drinks, were brought by waiters all in black. Neither Ari nor I took any. Ari, I saw, made sure to stay away from the king and queen. I wasn't sure why.

His energy stood out in the crowd. It wasn't just because I was in love with him. He had a regal bearing he had probably been taught to maintain his whole life until he was unaware of it. Even tense, he kept his chin high, his shoulders back. Though he didn't want it, and despite him not fitting in with his father's design, I could picture him in charge of it all some day, all the comings and goings of the Realm under his thumb. Would I be in that picture? I didn't know.

Finally the moment came when Ari was called to join his mother and father on the floating stage. They each had two escorts standing behind them. There was a banner of stars overhead. Winter wore all white. Kean was in purple and white. Ari stood more beautiful than anyone there, in silver and red with his unbound brown hair flowing behind him, his dark eyes catching glints of the perpetual dawn. My breath caught in my throat.

I stood to the side of the stage where Ari was, as close to him as I could get without actually being on the stage. Guards blocked me but I stayed as close as they'd allow.

Sullen stood with me, always formal. Always close.

Finally, everyone quieted. The king gave a signal and ten hawkships entered the dome tunnel, drifted slowly down through the air, and silently circled the proceedings before landing in a circle around us. They were stunning, silver sculpted ships, not big, but not small, like star-yachts that could accommodate a couple dozen crew each.

Each ship was slightly different, but they all had the shape and form of a hawk, their bows beaked with a downward curve. Where the tops of the wings would be, the shape curved outward, smooth and streamlined, then flared to where the wingtips would furl. The wings did not move. The ships were efficient, all of one piece, and I could see they would be swift in battle. Like fast darts. Like silver fish gliding through an airless black sea.

I'd never seen such a spectacle since the fleet of hummingbird ships was sent for me. And even then, only one of them landed in the yellow field outside the Temple to escort me away.

I remembered to take a breath as the ships settled, their lights flashing green and red all around us.

Kean began to speak and a hush fell, reverent, auspicious.

Such a big event. The biggest for these people in recent history. The fact that I was here as part of it all was amazing, and yet I was also the cause. The reason. This never would have happened so quickly if I had not healed the prince.

I could barely think, or concentrate, again hearing only every third word of the king's words. But the words didn't really matter. What mattered was what came afterward. What mattered was that these people might feel whole again, that everyone, like anxious Ari, could conceivably be healed so swiftly.

The dome's coloring was a purplish haze, and glimmered with a white sizzle like static. Beyond it was darkness except for the rising sun and the ever-following moons in orbit. Beyond that, the black of the net kept out the starlight, and the galaxy beyond.

When Kean finished his speech not a sound could be heard anywhere on the field. Even the holocams were silent.

He gave the signal with a lifting of his hand. All breathing seemed to stop. The black net that guarded the moons shimmered.

Then the barrier fell, a darkness vanishing upon a greater darkness.

It seemed all the stars rushed in at once, making my eyes tear.

I looked up and up. Beyond the dome appeared more shapes, iron-colored, bluish, with blinking lights.

The stars were laced with starships. Hawkships. Hummingbird ships. City ships. Round ships. Squares and triangles stretching outward, the furthest no more than flickering lights. All had come to be a part of the spectacle. Fleets beyond imagining. All the ships of the Realm.

They had been beyond the net waiting to show themselves for this moment of freedom, this moment when the Realm came back into the light. As the net completely dissolved, they flew over the landing field and above the dome in formation, five lines of ships by the hundreds moving swiftly north over the moon and into the waiting darkness beyond.

Now noise filled the field. Murmurs of awe and delight. For minutes, it lasted. The flight of the fleets, silent and steady, a display the likes of which I'd probably never see again.

Then I heard a crack. Perhaps fireworks to further display their pride?

But as I had that thought, I was flying forward fast, and something hit me hard in the face. I realized in a daze that it was the rough ground that had slammed into me. I had fallen, and something had landed square on top of me so I couldn't move, couldn't see.

Then I began to hear the screams.

There had only been that one crack, one pop, like an explosion. Only one. But the chaos that erupted grew like a wave.

I tried again to move, only to realize the thing on top of me was a man. I rolled, pushing at him, and saw with horror it was Sullen. His eyes were open, green and moisture-tinged. The side of his head, where there used to be braids, was open and red.

I cried out, but he was already dead. He had protected me by falling into me and taking the brunt of whatever had torn into his skull.

"Sullen." I grasped his arm. "No." My whole body was shaking. I wanted to yell, but only repeated noises escaped me, scratchy and low. "No, no, no."

I sat up, unharmed, trying to get my bearings, my hair in my face. Sullen rolled limp to my side. Another soft sound of grief escaped me and I started to reach out to Sullen. My hand cupped the side of his face. I started to pull him to me, crying out for help, my voice sounding lost in the depths of my throat.

Then I heard someone yelling. "The king! The king!" People were running toward me until I was surrounded by legs. Several hands came at me and grabbed me. I shrunk back until I realized they were trying to help me stand. Others were seeing to Sullen. But it was too late.

All I could think was, *Ari.*

Voices came at me all at once. "The healer! Tahir! Come quick," and before I could even comprehend what was happening I was being shoved and pulled to the stage. I saw smears of blood on the arms of my coat, my hands. Red. Sticky.

As I was being dragged up onto the stage, I looked outward, away from myself, my vision clearing.

A sudden crystal awareness came over me. Everything slowed. I saw Winter off to the side, her white robes splashed with red. Out my peripheral vision, I saw guards escorting people away. I saw other guards tussling with two large men, shoving them down to the ground. I saw blue-clad medics leaning over two bodies. One dressed in purple. One in red.

I pulled out of the grasping hands of the group of people yelling at me. "Ari!"

I ran across the platform, past the podium. Ari lay on his stomach, his coat shredded, his back exposed, torn and bleeding. He was not moving. Two medics were there with equipment I never used or understood, fastening things to his arms, hooking machines to his back.

As I came within five feet of him, several people held me back.

"Let me go! I can help him!" I realized I was yelling so loud my throat was being torn by my words.

"The king. You must go to the king!" Someone yelled into my ear.

"No!" My hair was tangled against my face, stinging my eyes, sticking to my cheeks. But I looked where they were pointing.

Kean lay on his side. There was blood everywhere on the ground beneath him. Four medics worked over him, but they were slow. The equipment was not being utilized as much, except for something gold being pressed to his neck. The two closest to his head were shaking their heads.

"The king!" I heard the voice again, then more voices all around me, pulling me away from Ari. "The king! You must help the king!"

I planted my feet. Tried to break their grasps and turn back toward Ari who looked so badly off and wasn't moving. I turned my head back and forth from Ari to Kean. A strange cry came from my throat. "Ari." The word emerged like a strained, garbled plea.

Then a voice at my ear said, "The king needs you more."

I lost all my strength. Hands forced me down toward Kean and I kept shaking my head, trying to protest. "Let me go to him!" The smell of blood like hot iron, tart and acrid, permeated the dry air.

Someone said, "He's right here." They didn't know I meant Ari.

"I can't," I heard myself say. "I'm not prepared. The wound is too serious."

"You have to try. He's the king!"

The medics backed off when they saw me being pushed to my knees at the king's side. One remained, putting pressure on the wound at Kean's neck. I could see the damage clearly now, jagged and deep, a long gash over the jugular. He'd already lost a massive amount of blood. We were kneeling in it, all of us surrounding him, the warmth of it soaking into the cloth at my

165

knees. The medics had the skin knitters out, and blood packs, but I could see they wouldn't finish in time. His heart would stop before they would be able to stabilize him. And even if they got his heart going again, he had lost too much blood. He had seconds left.

There was nothing else I could do. They wouldn't let me see Ari and Kean was right in front of me. Tears spilled from my eyes as I leaned down and put my lips to Kean's.

My gift woke but it was sleepy. My own panic and shock blocked it, a self-preservation technique that conserved energy for my own health and state of mind.

I pushed with my mind, giving it all I had left and finally the empathic gate opened, flooding my mind, finding its connection to my patient through lips and mouth and breath until the energy of our minds coalesced and spun.

Immediately, I saw Kean's lowered energy. He had almost nothing left to connect to. Like trying to find the last drops of a light rain in desert sand.

My energy pulled at whatever essence of Kean it could find, feeding into it, slowly at first, then faster, until I was pouring all I had into him.

Gold stars fell all around me turning to black ash. I could no longer feel his lips, but his body against mine was cold, too cold.

This was what I'd been hired to do. This was what I came here for. To obey the king. Help the king. Even my healing of the son was always and only for the king.

Now the falling stars were bigger flames crashing into me, wrapping me in soot and giant black flakes. I gave and gave until everything went black.

19

I had a dream I was shouting. "Let me be with him. Let me be with him!"

"No," they said.

The sky was falling.

Something soft cushioned my back. Hands touched me from above. I realized they were holding me down, holding my arms, bracing my kicking legs. My muscles ached as if I'd just run a long marathon all uphill.

Someone was screaming so loud it hurt my ears.

My throat was raw. Every breath I took was cold. Every exhale was like something crashing up through my lungs, scraping my throat, wrenching my mouth.

I tried to make words form. "Ari, Ari." But nothing happened. Just the screams again and again.

I thought of how he had been lying so still on that stage, face down and covered in blood. I thought about how, my back to him, I'd bent to the king, not fighting harder to go to Ari, not protesting enough. My duty. My heart. Before leaving the Temple, duty and heart had always been one and the same for me. When had everything changed?

I had another dream of total blackness, blindness. Nothing existed but I could still feel something of myself leftover, trying to claw through shiny, dark void.

For a long time I had that dream. My heart felt as if it had stopped. I didn't breathe.

It seemed years passed. Finally the darkness flickered just a little. I watched with no eyes, my entire body invisible to me. I couldn't help but be intrigued.

Flickers of gold. Orange. Red. Daffodils. Pumpkins. Roses.

A voice came and went. "Please come back." "Tahir." "Please hear me." "Tahir, you are wanted." "Tahir, you are needed."

A part of me thought it was Zash and I was back at the Temple recovering from a particularly energetic healing. I was young and still learning. I was eighteen and had failed my first real patient and run out of the room to my bed. Zash had found me there, too weary to move, trying not to sob like a baby. He told me, "This is one step of many. You are the most talented healer I've ever seen." He had smiled and that smile had gone straight to my heart like a warm light. "Sleep and when you wake you will be stronger and we will try again."

He never let me down. Zash was my confidant and my strength whenever I thought I was failing. I would think of that smile and my will would wake.

Now I saw him, a faded silhouette waving on the blackness.

The figure absorbed itself into the void, only to reveal another.

Ari was like a man on fire, all in red, so bright against the dark. His image came slowly closer until I could make out the silk scarves of plum, pink and lavender flowering all around him. His eyes shimmered, dark and wet. He was a god rising from the nothing. Sinarha, born of three suns, but heart of the dark. The final word in the story of Sinarha was always the same. *Remember.*

I heard a voice again by my ear. "Remember me. Come back."

A singularity of beauty moved through me. Seeing him. Hearing him. I saw rain and a child at a closed door. I saw bronze rivers and forests of emerald. I felt the love of a boy on dewy grass. I felt the hand of a father who was more father to me than my own. I tasted pain and sickness and turned it to gold dust to be scattered into the cosmos. I heard the whir of the hummingbird ship that had come to bear me away. Saw more stars than could possibly be counted in the vastness of one mind. Tasted their fire. Felt their heat. And one lonely star, a cast-off survivor of an unknown storm, lay beneath me and held me as I showed him my love.

"Ari." I spoke the word to the star-clustered reaches. And to the vision of a mythical god before me.

"Yes," it answered.

Suddenly I had a body. It opened its eyes. It reached up.

Ari was there, in a real room, sitting on the edge of a real bed. He took me into his arms.

20.

Snow drifted in gentle flutters against my face, mixing with my tears.

My body shivered. The cold air was numbing, good to feel now. Better than the hot indoors and all the heavy air.

I breathed in. My heart lightened even as it grew colder.

I sat on the edge of a long, metal chair, perhaps used during the endless summer days for sun-bathing. All around me the silence grew, thick and serene. The land was white all the way to the trees, which were dark and furry, evergreens sweeping a real sky with their paintbrush tops.

I wanted to bury myself in the snow. I wanted to live in the heart of the coldness for awhile because it seemed somehow so pure, yet evanescent. I wanted to hold onto it while I could, because nothing ever stayed the same.

I knew that now.

It was ironic that the funeral was on Darkquill, the very moon where we had wanted to go after the net came down. But that was where Sullen's family lived. The moon was actually where he'd been born.

I heard footsteps crunch behind me.

I sighed and did not turn. Quilted arms came around me. I leaned back into the strong embrace.

Ari said, breath warm on my ear, "You'll freeze to death. Come back in."

"I have this jacket you gave me. It's quite warm."

"Come on. A lot of the guests are already leaving. We should go, too."

"I need to say good bye to his kids. Tell them again what a great man he was."

"That's fine," he said softly.

I wanted Sullen's kids to know and remember clearly who their father was. I wanted them to hear it from me. Because maybe I was the one who had saved the king the day the net came down, but it was Sullen who had saved me. If he had not, Kean would be dead, I would be dead, and Ari's mind would most probably belong to the void itself.

Sullen would always be the hero in my mind. No one could ever tell me otherwise.

It had only been two days since the explosion. Three men had been immediately arrested. The explosion had been a singular act of violence, an internal affair. Disgruntled citizens turned terrorists. Part of the set-up crew for the ceremony on the moon base tarmac had planted a pulse bomb under the floating stage. Some thought they might have been the same three who had attacked me and never been apprehended. But I hadn't ever seen their faces. I would never know.

Ari had recovered quickly from his injuries. The medics saved his life, not me. I hadn't fought hard enough to get to him, and I would have to live with that for the rest of my life.

He did not remember the bomb, or anything of that day. Ari's last memory was getting up that morning and opening the curtains to let the light stir me awake.

I slept for twenty-four hours after healing the king. Actually, the king had died in my arms, but my healing of his body had given the medics extra time to revive him. When they re-started his heart, they told me he sat up, body whole again, looking around and wondering why he was lying on the stage. He had needed no recovery time. Due to me, his health and strength returned with even more vigor than before.

Some thought I would not wake at all after I lost consciousness. The medics thought I was in a coma but their machines would not confirm it. In truth, I was merely asleep, so they kept me hydrated, watched over me. My new escorts told me Ari never left my side.

When I finally awakened, I had felt tired, but fine. I clung to Ari's hand for hours afterward, and would not let him go.

Ari filled me in on what had happened. Everything he had learned. He told me about the funeral for Sullen and said we could go. He said he knew I'd want that. He already had a hummingbird ship waiting. Even though we both still needed more rest, we packed within hours of my waking, and left with the king's blessing.

The voyage took six hours, during which we slept some more.

When the ship landed, it was snowing. We made our way through frosted ground into the family compound to a suite that was waiting for us.

The next day was the funeral.

Only now, here in the sweetness of Darkquill's winter, with the edge of the forest breathing close, did I finally feel the numbness in my limbs begin to recede.

Ari held out his hand. I took it and stood. Together we walked inside to where all the friends and family of Sullen had gathered.

Epilog

After we left the gathering for Sullen, we returned to our suite in the Darkquill compound. The front room had a flowery mural on one wall, not frilly, but painted all in black and white and gray shades. The curtains were emerald green and made of some sort of soft material that draped exquisitely. A lamp with a round, green glass the exact shade of the curtains sat on a low table. It looked like a green moon amidst shadows of black and tarnished silver. Other walls had recessed shelves carved into the walls, and arches over those shelves with trees on top and ivy carved about their borders from floor to ceiling. There were black leather couches and chairs, low tables made of glass with trinkets on them that flashed, not decorative alone, but media devices, balls that spit out holograms, screens that floated and grew in size at a touch. There was a wooden desk in one corner, with a chair and another green lamp.

The ceilings were tall and arched. A round, crystal chandelier hung in the center of it all.

When we had first arrived, Ari smiled at me and said, "Your mouth is hanging open. Wait until you see the bedroom."

Our bedroom now. It was red and black. Ari's colors, of course. The room was huge enough to be a single apartment. The walls were painted in uneven, square shapes of silver, white, black and red. The darker colors did not make the room look shadowed, but actually brightened it. Red candles sat on the bed tables. There were two more couches, both red, and curtains of silver, like worked metal, but thin, opaque.

The bed itself was supported on a large black frame that had thick posts carved like castle towers. The posts held aloft a sweeping, solid black canopy. The design was like a little mini-castle carved of marble. The headboard was cushioned red velvet. The covers on the bed were red and black satin. The entire concoction looked like a nest of royal tastes combined with the beauty of sculpture, and comfort for the weary.

Upon first entering the room, I couldn't look away for long minutes.

Now I lay back against the red velvet, with the black canopy overhead, the satin comforter over me. All was peaceful, quiet, safe. Yet I was still overwhelmed by everything from the past two days.

Ari lay beside me on his side, head propped against the pillows.

The Realm was free of its protective net now, but we didn't talk of that. Instead, he leaned in and his lips brushed against my cheek. I reached for his hand.

Slowly, he moved over me, his body sliding warm against mine, and it was all I wanted now. His lips moved to mine, wine-sweet. I put my arms around him and caressed his back. His back. Which had been shredded and bloody only two days ago, now seamless, smooth. Repaired to perfection. But not by me.

I shut my eyes hard against that memory but not soon enough. Against his lips, my sobs broke free.

Ari pulled back. "Tahir?"

"I should have gone to you. To you, not the king." It was the first time I'd said anything to him about my feelings concerning that. We'd been focused more on Sullen for the last day.

I opened my eyes to look into his face. Ari's sleek eyebrows moved together. "But I'm fine. And Kean wouldn't have been."

I nodded. Took a breath, but my chest heaved. I couldn't speak.

Ari brushed at my swiftly falling tears. "You did everything you could. And beyond. We lost good people, one councilor, two escorts. You are grieving for Sullen, I know—"

I let out an exasperated groan and sat forward, pushing him up and off me. He rolled to the side and I followed, looming over him. "It's not only about that!" My words came harsher than I'd expected.

I pushed him down and he did not resist. He looked up at me, blinking as if clueless, and I gripped him by the shoulders and shook him. Hard. "You can't do this to me. You have to give me permission to use the gift at any time I feel is right. You can't make me stumble around wondering, or have doubts in my mind that take precious time to decipher. If anything happens to you, I have to be able to help without second thoughts."

"If you had fought harder to come to me," said Ari, "my father would not still be alive. Besides, from what I heard, you didn't have a choice. You were forced to the king's side by his entourage."

"But I tried to go to you. I want you to understand that."

"I do. But you have to understand that my father needed you more. Why are you feeling guilty over that?"

"Because I didn't know that. I didn't know you weren't as close to death as he was. No one knew that at the time!"

"Yes, Tahir, they did."

"I can't live like this, not able to use my gift if you really need it. Not able to make my own choices. Only directed by the king. By his entourage."

"Then who decides the definition of 'need'?"

"I will!"

"In a case like this, you were incapable. You didn't see the explosion. You didn't see what happened."

I gripped his shoulders hard until I felt my fingernails dig in to his skin. He didn't flinch.

"That's exactly why I'm upset. I didn't know you would be all right. And I don't want you to think I didn't choose you first!"

"I don't." He pulled his hand from between us and cupped my cheek.

Tears slipped quickly from my eyes again, before I even realized it. My cheeks felt hot under the trickle of liquid. "You have to trust me. You have to let me be the one to know when it is right to help you, and when it is not. If you can't, I will—I will—" I couldn't finish.

"Leave?" he asked.

"It was too hard. When I saw you both lying there, I broke apart. I thought I'd be useless anyway, because of how I felt. I wasn't prepared. My gift was not prepared. When they took me away from you I couldn't breathe. I couldn't feel my own body. Even as I sat beside your father and everyone urged me on, I couldn't feel a thing. The healing. Making his body heal, feeling for his heart. One minute to the next he was dying, then he was dead. I don't remember the medics restarting his heart. I don't remember a thing about it except the kiss. And how much I only wanted it to be you. I thought I had failed you both, in every way!"

Unseeing, my throat choked, the words stuttering. I felt his arms go around me and tighten. My wet cheek rested against the silk of his shoulder.

I heard him say, "You didn't fail, Tahir. You've never failed any of us yet. And even now you're being revered by the court, the press, the public. You won't be able to go anywhere for a long time without being mobbed."

"Great." But I felt my lips curve up a fraction.

Ari said, "And if the promise you made to me not to take away the pain of my grief feels like a burden to you, well, it shouldn't. I have to do this emotional stuff my own way. I have to use all of it to learn and grow. My emotions, whether they are a turmoil to me, to others, or to the whole Realm, are mine. It's how I am. With everything I've gone through, everything I'm feeling, I have to believe I'll be stronger for it for the future."

"But what if I see you suffering and make another mistake? Will you hate me?"

"I didn't hate you before."

"Oh." I exhaled loudly. "I couldn't tell."

"My stress before the ceremony wasn't for you. Or about you."

I could smell the salt of my tears, taste them on my lips. I felt him take a deep breath before continuing.

"Tahir." Ari stopped. His lips were against my forehead. "I could never hate you. Don't you know I love you?"

It was the first time I'd heard him say those words.

He added, "Didn't you see any of that when your gift touched my mind?"

But it didn't work that way. The gift never worked that way, or in any straight-forward manner of mind-reading. The connection we'd had when Arku had been there had come partially from the effects of the splinter-bomb on both of us. That was an isolated event, the way we could see ourselves and communicate with each other telepathically. Most of the time the gift did not facilitate easy, back and forth communication at all. What we had experienced was special.

"I saw only what my gift wanted to heal. The good things? That is not what my gift seeks out. It doesn't take away pleasure, goodness, happiness. Love."

"That's good to know." His hands pressed the sides of my head. "Very good."

I looked at him, blinking, still hearing those words he'd never said before. *I love you.*

Expression open but insistent, he began, "Tahir, I—"

"You know I love you, too, don't you?" I interrupted.

The smile that touched his lips was reverent, tender. We stared at each other until it almost became uncomfortable. Then he said, voice a little shaky, "Did you know I made my father name one of the hawkships after you?"

"What?"

"Yeah."

"When was this?"

"The day before the ceremony. He argued with me a little, but in the end he just did it. I think he agreed to it so I would leave him alone."

I laughed. "It's a weapon, you know."

"I know. You're disappointed, right?"

176

"No." I kissed him. "No. Ari, I've never been disappointed in you. Not for one single moment from the first day I met you."

He pulled back. "The first day you met me I wanted to kill you."

"Well," I said. "You know what they say. There's a very fine line between love and hate."

He laughed out loud. "You are the most incredible person I've ever met."

Those words were like a wind of warm stars surrounding me, drying the emptiness of my tears, filling me up. It all felt like some rushing dream, but we had created it. Together. I wanted to go forward with him now. Build a life. I felt he was ready.

We both were.

Ari leaned in to kiss me. Our lips met, solid and warm.

The stars had returned.

THE END

Dear Reader:

Thank you for reading. I hope you enjoyed Ari and Tahir as much as I enjoyed writing about them and their gloomy, gilt and gothic moon.

The Moonling Prince 1 and 2 both take place in a self-created milieu I call my far future Starshiptopian universe where there is a starship around every corner, a human colonized galaxy, and realms galore to explore.

Other books of mine that take place in my Starshiptopia include:

Letters to an Android
Scoundrel
Eve of the Great Frost (novella published by Mischief Corner Press in the 2016 Christmas anthology "This Wish Tonight")
The Android and the Thief (April 2017 from Dreamspinner Press)

I am at work on another Starshiptopian novel tentatively titled *Lake in the Stars* and hope to have it out in 2017.

Feel free to follow my author page on Amazon:
https://www.amazon.com/Wendy-Rathbone/e/B00B0O9BMS/ref=dp_byline_cont_book_1
Or "friend" me on Facebook:
https://www.facebook.com/wendy.rathbone.3
You can also follow my blog at:
http://wendyrathbone.blogspot.com/
I often post updates, free giveaways, poetry and more.

All my self-pubbed books are available from:
www.eyescrypublications.com.

Wendy Rathbone

Since the mid-'80s Wendy Rathbone has had over 500 poems published in both mainstream and genre venues. She's had seven chapbooks published from seven different publishers and recently they were all gathered together in an omnibus edition, "Unearthly," available on Kindle from Amazon which also includes her first place award-winning chapbook "Scrying the River Styx" from the Anamnesis Press chapbook contest.

Wendy has been nominated over a dozen times for the Science Fiction Poetry Association's Rhysling Award, and for their Dwarf Star short-short poetry award. Her most recent work can be found in: Asimov's SF, Pedestal Magazine, Dreams and Nightmares, Scifikuest, Horror Writers of America Poetry Showcase, One Sentence Poems, Mythic Delirium, and more.

A brand new short story, "I Keep the Dark That is Your Pain," is also out in the pivotal 2015 anthology: A Darke Phantastique.

Her soft sf novel "Letters to an Android" is on Amazon Kindle and in paperback; it is a book of festering green skies, haiku, star boats and emotional androids.

Wendy is also the author of the scifi novel "Pale Zenith" (Eye Scry Publications) and its accompanying two-story volume, "Moltenrose." Her short story collection, "Beneath the Blue Dusk and the Sea" is also just out, as well as several male/male romances including a vampire-fairy novel, "Lace." She lives in the high desert of Yucca Valley, CA with her partner of 35 years, three dogs and three cats. She talks about writing and does mini-interviews with other authors at her blog, "From the Left Dimension"...
http://wendyrathbone.blogspot.com

Turn Left at November

Poems by
Wendy Rathbone

Visit realms of diamond rain, dust-folk lands and valleys of curses and shame. Reside in the burning moonships of dream, the silt of stars, the asphyxiation of the waking day. Meet the golden android who houses your soul. Journey through tatters of stardust down roads of sorrow. Find hope in planets of candles and crazy-eyed mermen. There you will meet November in these rich and evocative poems by Wendy Rathbone.

Unmaking Autumn

Out at the excavation site
where they are taking apart autumn
leaf by fabled leaf
the searchlights try to catch us
putting the eyes back into the pumpkins
the moon back in the witch-shaped sky
We steal blood kisses
behind the naked apple orchards

LETTERS TO AN ANDROID

Wendy Rathbone

Cobalt is a created human, vat grown and born adult, with no human rights and indentured to serve others for the duration of his life. Liyan is a young man with wanderlust in his eyes, embarking on a career that takes him to the furthest regions of space. The two become unlikely friends and create a memorable long-distance correspondence. Through Liyan, Cobalt gets to explore the universe, living vicariously through his friend's wave transmissions. A strong bond develops between them that not even the stars can put asunder.

Now you know an android who writes poetry.

This is all your fault. Did you not read my last wave telling you extracurricular activities for my kind are discouraged? Of course this is harmless and strangely enjoyable and does not necessarily require me to leave the hotel. Pel would not care if I wrote lines of equations or nonsensical juxtaposed words. As long as the act does not bring my mental state into question.

However, in history, poetry is often written by the rebels.

So we can keep this to ourselves.

Let me know about your lieutenant's test.

And to give you peace of mind, I never believed you observed me as anything other than human.

Some people are and always will be hateful bigots. Most people are simply uncomfortable in speaking to "property." And anyway, friendship, like poetry, is also discouraged.

Your friend,
Cobalt

FROM THE AUTHOR:
www.eyescrypublications.com

ON AMAZON:
http://www.amazon.com/Letters-Android-Wendy-Rathbone/dp/0989693872/

SCOUNDREL
Wendy Rathbone
A male/male romance

Antares is a willing sex slave, trained in the harems of Anada since the age of 18, and owned by a wealthy master who spoils his slaves. But all that changes when Empire soldiers invade Antares' world and he is taken away from the only life he's ever known.

In a colonized galaxy where starships are as common as houseflies, and a dark Empire seeks to control thousands of civilized worlds, there are those who fall through the cracks and refuse to be conquered, including the pirate, Slate, and his crew.

Out in the darkness of the unknown, among Empire soldiers and scoundrels, will bad fates befall Antares and his fellow captive companions?

Will Slate finally find the love he's been looking for his whole life?

Can Slate and Antares ever see eye to eye?

A male/male romance to end all male/male romances!

FROM THE AUTHOR
www.eyescrypublications.com

ON AMAZON
http://www.amazon.com/Scoundrel-Wendy-Rathbone-ebook/dp/B014BU7V42/ref=sr_1_1?s=books&ie=UTF8&qid=1440660148&sr=1-1&keywords=scoundrel+wendy+rathbone

PALE ZENITH
Wendy Rathbone
A Science Fiction Novel

On a far-flung "Earth" in a parallel universe, two factions are fighting a decades-long psychic war. Young talented psychics are being temporarily kidnapped from present day Earth, seemingly at random, to serve as part of one side's psychic army. They are put under the control of spychiatrists, mysterious machines with many limbs that have a programmed ability to travel time and space and universes to kidnap and control carefully selected humans. The humans never know they are being used; when their missions are completed they are brought back to their universe through time and placed back in their beds, their memories wiped.

————————————

The shadows wound the tall corridor in muted gold, varnished brown. It seemed as though they were in the bowels of a giant serpent coiled outside time, outside space.

When they left the palace, a familiar sun flourished in a clear, blue sky. But this wasn't their sun. Not Zack's sun. It was an alien star burning within a different galaxy in an all too distant universe. Zack looked up squinting, trying to see if he could peer beyond the sky, beyond the pale of midday and into his own timespace, but there was nothing. Only sunlight. Only the thin atmosphere of an Earth not his own.

His back knotted again. Leo's presence was a gelid space inside his chest, empty. Always before he'd felt a warmth there, a sort of pressure like someone's hand pressed gently to his heart. He'd taken Leo for granted knowing, the way a shadow falls when you block the sun, that he was there around him, inside him: blood, air, salt, brain, soul. They were genetic duplicates, twins, spiritual halves. Without him, Zack knew the first icy tugs of panic.

FROM THE AUTHOR
www.eyescrypublications.com

ON AMAZON
Pale Zenith

183

The Foundling
by Wendy Rathbone

Diego is a powerful man with a tragic past. Out on the expansive ocean in his private yacht, he discovers a beautiful and mysterious man adrift on a raft, near death. The bond that forms between them in the aftermath of Alec's rescue is one of fierce passion, though lacking in trust. Can they make it work, or will Alec's amnesia bring forth secrets so disturbing as to tear them apart? A passionately erotic love story of desire and darkness, exquisite and explicit.

_____

I can see his struggle between gratitude and uneasiness. He is buffeted by all things new and strange. He does not know where he is from, who he is or what happened to him. He does not know me. There has not been enough time to transition between strangers and friendship.

This isolation of his is something I can identify with, but it is also a feeling no one can help him with until or unless he gets his own life back. And his memory.

If that doesn't happen, then it will take time for him to build a new life. He is polite to me, even friendly, but even a night together during a storm with his arms wrapped tight around my waist doesn't calm the surge I see inside him, the emptiness, the loss, possibly even panic. That night may have reinforced some trust in me, but so far not enough for him to completely relax.

He seeks me out, though. That's something. He sits by me at dinner when he can have any seat of his choosing. I watch him closely when he does not realize it. At dinner the following night after we had only 'slept' together, and before we go to bed again in separate rooms, I notice everything about him, how he moves, the way the air warms when he is closer to me, the dry sheen of his lips as they part for more air when he is reacting to something, or speaking, or eating.

His hands still shake. Anyone else might not notice because he keeps them clasped into fists at his sides or, while sitting, pressed tight to his lap.

I spend another fretful night alone. I dream restlessly, wild, loud and colorful visions I cannot recall at all as soon as my eyes open. All I know is the dreams leave me unfulfilled, impatient.

www.eyescry.com/html/publications.htm

Other fiction titles from Eye Scry Publications...

SONS OF NEVERLAND
an erotic vampyre novel
by Della Van Hise

"The virtuosity shown here is only the beginning of a pyrotechnic talent unfolding into the hidden dimensions of the human and nonhuman spirit."
-Jacqueline Lichtenberg

"What *Sons of Neverland* resembled to me was the creative hagiographies of Nikos Kazantzakis, where a few stylized characters deliver a message that goes way beyond the parameter of the characters themselves. And much like Kazantzakis, this book zones on the question of immortality. However, this is not just the decadent historical immortality of the long-lived vampire, it is immortality as a change in one's perception. This is the story behind the story, delivered by characters that are hyper-real - each one loaded with symbolism. Sons of Neverland will have you filled, even brimming over with the sense of Mysterium Tremendum et Fascinans. Go there for a full helping of the numinous." (A Reviewer on Amazon)

Set against a backdrop of contemporary culture, SONS OF NEVERLAND explores the universal questions of life & death, sex & love - the most crucial challenges every human being faces - through the eyes of the immortal vampire.

The novella "Kiss of the Black Angel" is available for free on Kindle – a preview to SONS OF NEVERLAND.

www.eyescrypublications.com

185

"If Prince of Umberlight doesn't rattle your cage, you're more dead than the undead!" **-Night Readers**

Thorn may be an 800 year old vampire, but he does not possess the ability to create others of his kind, and so he is cursed to fall in love with mortals, only to watch them grow old and die. Torn by grief, Thorn denounces his immortality and enters into a comatose oblivion for decades. When he awakens, he is no longer in London, but finds himself in a world spun into being by his own desires - a world where Time and Death do not exist, a world where it is forever autumn, where the Parish of Shadows and the River of Stars become his home. It is in this world of Umberlight that he meets Atom - an interloper into his private sanctuary, but also an impudent imp who is destined to reveal to Thorn the three dangerous elements a vampire must possess in order to become a Creator.

The Art of Brutality.
Submission to Dark Desire.
Love.

FROM THE AUTHOR
www.eyescrypublications.com

ON AMAZON
http://www.amazon.com/Prince-Umberlight-Tales-Book-ebook/dp/B00TRD2EHS/ref=asap_bc?ie=UTF8

YEAR OF THE RAM
Della Van Hise

Year of the Ram was described by one reviewer as... "A spacefaring gay romance full of love, angst, and longing."

Only after Star Commander Morgan Diego becomes an exile as a result of a Galaxy Corps political blunder does he begin to realize how much he valued the companionship of his second in command - the mysterious Lucien, an Alfarian who is more elven than human, with peculiar powers & abilities which begin to unfold as he, too, realizes what he has lost.

Separated by circumstance from his former life, Morgan is thrust into a world where he must survive by his wits. When he meets a peculiar little old man calling himself Kim Le, Morgan finds himself in a situation where he is required to master The Art - not only a form of human & extraterrestrial martial arts, but a way of living and being that will alter his life forever.

At the temple, he is introduced to his new teacher, another Alfarian who begins to steal his heart - a heart which is already promised to Lucien. Torn and conflicted, Morgan struggles with the world he left behind and the world he now inhabits.

Beginning to believe he may never again return to his ship and to the friends and loved ones he left behind, he is all the more frustrated and heartbroken when a new Master arrives at the temple: a man to whom Morgan is immediately drawn both mentally and physically, a man who is strikingly familiar... yet utterly alien.

Year of the Ram is a fully-fleshed novel, approximately 97000 words, with a focus on the love story and romance angle. Set against a science fiction milieu, it explores the infinite possibilities of the human and alien heart. Sexual content is explicit, though is not the primary focus of the novel.

For those who like a romance that forces its characters to contemplate the ecstasies AND the agonies of love... you will enjoy *Year of the Ram* immensely.

FROM THE AUTHOR:
www.eyescrypublications.com
ON AMAZON:
http://www.amazon.com/Year-Ram-Della-Van-Hise/dp/0989693813/

All of our titles are available directly from our website, on Amazon, or may be ordered from most booksellers. Thanks for reading us!

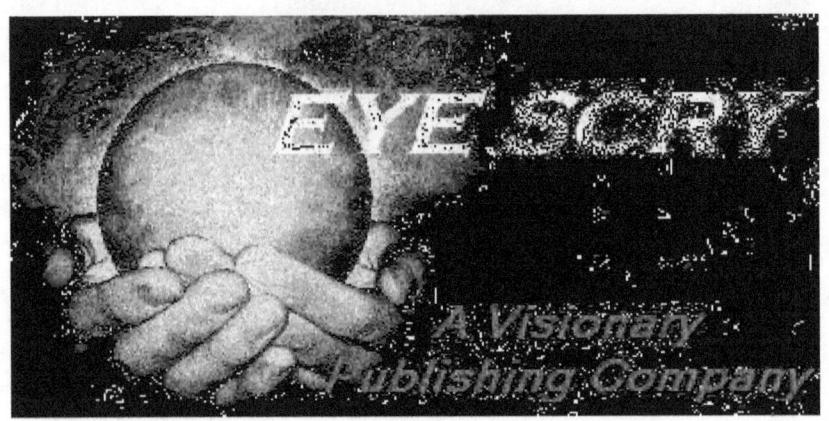

Eye Scry Publications
A Visionary Publishing Company
www.eyescrypublications.com